OMEGA SHARED

BOOK FOUR OF THE NORTHERN LODGE PACK SERIES

SUSI HAWKE

AN M/PREG PARANORMAL ROMANCE

What happens when your fated mate is also your natural predator?

Join my mailing list and get your FREE copy of The Rabbit Chase

https://dl.bookfunnel.com/vfk1sa9pu3

Twitter:
https://twitter.com/SusiHawkeAuthor

Facebook:
https://www.facebook.com/SusiHawkeAuthor

Alpha's Dream: Book 1

Non-Shifter Contemporary Mpreg

Pumpkin Spiced Omega: The Hollydale Omegas - Book 1

Cinnamon Spiced Omega: The Hollydale Omegas - Book 2

Peppermint Spiced Omega: The Hollydale Omegas - Book 3

CHAPTER 1

ZANE

The sight of the two large alphas kissing each other, locked in a furious embrace as they seemingly battled for dominance, was the hottest thing that I had ever seen in my life. I stood there, transfixed by the passionate sight and the heady scent of arousal that wafted through the air.

I came back to myself with a start as I realized that, once again, I was the awkward man on the outside looking in. And this time, I was acting like a stalker by standing here gaping and invading the privacy of these two men.

Horrified by my behavior, I spun around to go back the way that I had come. I hadn't made it three steps before the sound of a twig snapping under my foot echoed loudly through the surrounding woods.

Crap! Panicked, I took off running to get myself far away. Seconds later, I heard the sound of thundering footprints chasing me down. Zigzagging my way downhill, I tripped over my own feet, and went somersaulting for about twenty yards, only stopping when I painfully slammed up against the trunk of a large pine tree.

I sat there under the tree, catching my breath and picking needles out of my clothes and hair, when a large gray wolf jumped right in front of me, growling low in his throat.

Cowering, I held my hands up, palms out, and tilted my head to the side to offer my neck in submission to the alpha.

He sniffed the air around me, then morphed into a familiar face from my pack. His name was Owen, and he was a personal friend to the Alpha. Other than that, I didn't know much about the gorgeous mystery man. Except for the fact that I was really digging that spicy cinnamon stick smell of his.

He didn't hang out with us omegas much, except for meals. The rest of the time he spent patrolling our woods in his role as a pack guardian, or catching a few hours' sleep in his bunk on the third floor dormitory of the lodge that we all shared.

Arms crossed over his chest, he glared down at me. I was nearly choking from the angry pheromones he was putting out there, and didn't hear him when he spoke to me the first time.

"I'll ask you again. What the hell is an unmated omega

doing waltzing around my woods unescorted, and why the fuck were you spying on me?"

My anxiety spiked higher, and my vision began to blur around the edges, as if a million fuzzy pixels were framing my view of the world. Hugging myself, I rocked back and forth, trying to breathe, and completely unable to answer him, when I felt a strange tongue lick my ear.

Shocked by the intrusion, I jerked my head to the side to find a huge bear standing over me. At this point, I was shaking so hard that my teeth were clattering together. I almost passed out when the bear shifted into a large, kind looking man. He reached out and firmly gripped the back of my neck, sending out calming alpha pheromones in a strong wave that immediately calmed me.

"Now, if you're done freaking out, maybe you can answer my question?" Owen spoke impatiently, his rough voice edging on a growl.

"That will be enough for now, Owen," the huge, blonde bear man said firmly. His kind grayish-green eyes flashed with frustration, but his sweet coconut scent showed that he remained calm. "I think that we have perhaps traumatized the young omega enough for now, yes?"

Owen raked a hand through his thick head of wavy auburn red hair. His own green eyes sparked with fear as he spoke. "Traumatized *him*? *He's* the one who was fucking spying on *us*! I was just asking him what the hell he was doing. An omega like him shouldn't be out here alone anyway. It's not safe."

"It seems to me that he was safe enough to walk unaccompanied through his own territory. That is, until an alpha from his own pack decided to frighten him half to death. Obviously, he chanced upon us by happenstance, yes?"

Hearing his odd yet proper way of speaking sparked a memory of the day I'd first arrived here. Gasping, I turned to the man and smiled. "I remember you now. You're the guy that helped Micah with our flat tire the day that we came here! I can't believe that I didn't recognize you sooner."

He smiled, the hand on my neck relaxing and coming to rest on my shoulder. "Yes, my young omega friend. That was indeed me, although you cannot be blamed for not recognizing me. I had a beard then, but now I do not."

"Well, I've never been able to grow facial hair aside from random scruff, so I definitely would've remembered you if you still had that cool beard."

He smiled. "I am Karl, it is nice to see you again." Sniffing, he said, "You smell more mature now. You still have that sweet scent of gingersnaps about you, but it is much stronger now, yes?"

Laughing, I said, "Seriously? You're saying that I'm a ginger who smells like frigging gingersnaps to you? That's such cheesy irony!"

The warmth of his rolling laugh sent a flare of heat through my body. I licked my lips nervously, about to introduce myself, when Owen's annoyed voice interrupted our conversation.

"Yeah, yeah. The cute little omega twink smells like spicy cookies. Yada, yada. Back to my earlier questions, Zion. What are you doing out here alone, and why were you spying on us?"

My relaxed state flipped instantly to irritation. "First of all, the name is Zane. Which you should know, being that we've been in the same pack for almost two and a half years. Second, I was not spying on you. I was taking a walk through the woods, *an activity that was approved by our Alpha*, if you really must know. And third? Karl was right. I accidentally happened on to you guys, and I was leaving to give you privacy when you started chasing me like a predator."

Owen's stance relaxed slightly, and he flushed with embarrassment. "Fine. I won't say anything bad against Jake, but I will be asking him if he had intended for you to be out this far."

Oh, hell no. My ginger ire was definitely engaged now. "Seriously? That's fine, Owen. Whatever. I don't give a crap. Check up on me. But be ready for me to answer Alpha honestly when he asks me later if there was a reason for your concern. I'm not the one with anything to hide."

Flashing an apologetic look at Karl, I added with a sneer: "I mean, was there an actual reason that you should be concerned? Hmm, Owen? Is there danger out here in our pack woods? Or, are you maybe just afraid of the pack learning about your secret love life?"

Gritting his teeth, Owen leaned over and grabbed my chin. The shock in his eyes mirrored what I was feeling, as a jolt of electricity passed between us. He quickly dropped his hand, but said, "Don't think of threatening me, pup. I don't need to explain my concerns or reservations to you. Just keep your trap shut, and we'll be fine."

"Owen. That will be enough now," Karl commanded gently. "I believe that this interaction has gotten out of hand. We haven't even asked the omega if he was injured in his fall."

Blushing, I mumbled, "Zane. Please, my name is Zane. Not omega, and definitely not pup. And yeah, I'm okay. Just embarrassed, but that's normal for a klutz like me."

Karl looked at me gently, saying, "My sweet Zane. Please do not call yourself a klutz. I find that an abhorrent word to describe a delightful young man such as yourself."

After that, Karl patted my shoulder as he stood and then walked over to stand beside Owen. Looking back at me, he said, " Excuse us for a few minutes, Zane. I do apologize, but I believe that it is time for my friend, Owen, and I to have a private conversation. If you do not mind?"

I nodded, not sure how to respond with Owen still

glaring at me. *Whatever, dude.* Standing to my feet, I glared back and threw as much shade as I could muster, sneering at him with narrowed eyes.

He rolled his eyes and blew out an exasperated puff of air, but allowed Karl to pull him off into the trees to talk. That was my opening, and I took it. Quietly stepping around the tree, I quickly made a beeline for home, watching for stray twigs that would broadcast my movements to the alphas.

Once I felt that I was safely away, I broke into a run, not slowing down until I reached the lodge. I was relieved when I went inside and there was nobody around in the main living area. I went straight upstairs and headed to my bunk in the omega part of the dorms.

Flopping down on my back, I lay there panting for breath, while my heart-rate slowed down to normal. I pushed aside my strange attraction to the sweet bear for now, because after all, who had ever heard of a bear mating a wolf? I had a harder time ignoring the equally strong attraction I'd felt to that jerk, Owen.

I'd noticed him before, I mean, who wouldn't? He was the hot kind of red head, with the dark auburn hair and skin that actually tanned instead of burning at the slightest hint of sunshine. And that scent of his! How had I never noticed his scent before? It was just so... yummy.

My mind kept going back to Karl though. I mean, dang. He was easily a head taller than Owen, which was saying a lot. And that muscular body! I could spend days just tracing the lines of his ripped body, and still probably not be able to properly appreciate it. And was that a tattoo I'd seen on that juicy butt-cheek? I wish I'd had the courage to stare, and really drink him in.

But that wouldn't have been proper. Nudity is no big deal among shifters; we all have to strip to change, so it's just natural. Staring, however, is just bad manners. Such a shame. I could smell his coconut scent on my shoulder, where Karl had rested his hand.

I really needed to let the fantasy of the two alphas go, though. They were obviously a couple, which was oddly intriguing and sexy as heck. Probably taboo? I couldn't really say though. Just because I'd never heard of two alphas being involved or mixed species relationships before, didn't mean that either one wasn't a thing. I mean, what did I know? I was just an omega from a small pack.

CHAPTER 2

OWEN

"You know that the little twerp is getting away while we're over here talking, right?" I scowled at Karl, pissed off at the direction that our afternoon had gone.

"I am aware. That is why I wished for us to step away. It was the only way to afford him the dignity of escaping a situation that was embarrassing him and causing him distress."

Narrowing my gaze, I snarled at my long-time lover. "You like him. Don't even try to deny it, I can smell the interest all over you."

"I have always found his scent to be intriguing, since the day he arrived here in the presence of the alpha with the flattened tire. I cannot ignore that delectable scent of spicy cookies."

"I'm not gonna deny that the boy smells sweet as sugar. Doesn't matter, anyway. He's still an omega and I'm not looking to start a family."

"Owen. Zane is hardly a boy. I would judge him to be about twenty to twenty-three. That is roughly five to seven years younger than you or me. You must stop thinking of him as a child, simply because he is an omega. That is not very enlightened of you, my love."

Rolling my eyes, I reached out to rest my hand on his hip and pull him closer to me. "Are you trying to replace me, Karl? Is this you telling me that our time together is up?"

Karl cupped my face in his big hands and touched his forehead to mine. "Owen. Why must I constantly be forced to assure you of my love? No. Today we will not argue. It is not the time to discuss our young omega friend right now. Instead, we focus on us, yes?"

With a light sigh, I nodded my head. I hated it when we argued, especially when I knew it was because I was being an asshole. Again.

Karl's lips touched mine then, softly then with a little more pressure as I started to kiss him back. The way his large body towered over and wrapped around mine really excited me. It was such a turn-on, knowing I could easily be overpowered by this huge man, when I was used to being the big guy in the room.

I was as much of an alpha as the next guy, but when I was

with Karl, I couldn't deny the simple pleasure of not always needing to be the one in control. Not that I was submissive to him, it wasn't like that at all. We balanced each other. Where I tended to be ruled by my emotions, Karl was calm and logical. We took turns being in charge, and it worked well for us.

I wished I knew how to tell my pack about my lover, and permanently claim him as my mate. I just didn't know if my pack would accept our relationship, not that I gave a shit. But I just didn't want Karl hurt. Not only was Karl a bear shifter, and not a wolf, he was also another alpha. I was pretty sure that the whole thing would scandalize my friends. When I finally told them. Which I knew I would at some point.

Karl deserved more than a boyfriend who hid him in the woods like a dirty little secret. I didn't even know what an actual relationship between two alphas would entail on a day to day basis, or where we would even live. His den? My pack? The lodge? One of the unused cabins on the property?

These were all things that we needed to discuss before we could move forward. I just was't sure how to express all of this to Karl without freaking him out and sounding like an asshole. All I knew was that it'd been getting harder and harder to kiss him good-bye and go home alone every night.

His teeth scraped against my alpha gland, sending an electric surge straight to my cock. My head rolled back as

I bared my neck to him further, yielding myself to the other alpha.

"Mmm, you are being a very good boy, Owen. Perhaps I should offer a reward, yes?" His hand moved down to wrap around our cocks, rubbing his up against mine as he spoke.

"Fuuuck, yeah," I moaned. "Like that, Karl."

Our heads touched as we looked down to watch our cocks slide against each other in the grip of his big, strong hand. The heads were pushing through the opening in his fist with each thrust of our hips. Both of us had fat pearls of thick white juice seeping through our slits that mixed together when the thick mushroom heads pushed through the opening.

I wanted nothing more than to taste that combination of our flavors, so I reached out a thumb and scooped some up, rubbing it across my lips. Karl's pupils dilated as he watched me. Another scoop, and I spread a matching glaze across his lips too.

With a growl, he leaned over to mash his lips against mine. Walking me backwards, he pinned me against a tree and kissed the fuck out of me. The taste of our salty pre-cum coated our tongues now as they wrestled against each other in my mouth.

Breaking away, Karl released his grip on our cocks, and stepped away. Running a hand through his thick blonde hair, he gasped out, "Please. Give me a moment. I do not wish for it to end quickly like this today."

Leaning back against the tree, I raised a brow as I licked my lips. My hand was slowly stroking my rock-hard cock in a leisurely pace, teasing Karl as he watched, his own hand squeezing the root of his cock in a white-knuckled grip.

"And how exactly would you like to end things today, big guy? Would you like me to bend over, or shall I shove you to the ground and fill your ass with my seed? Your choice, babe."

Wordlessly, Karl turned around and dropped to the ground. Lowering himself onto all fours, presenting himself to me, he looked back at me over his shoulder as he wiggled his ass enticingly.

Kneeling down, I ran my tongue along his crack, stopping to lap around his fluttering hole. There wasn't much time; my throbbing need wouldn't allow me to wait long, but I needed to get some moisture there.

"Please. Just put it inside me, my love," Karl groaned, "I cannot wait much longer."

Pulling myself up onto my knees, I spat in my hand and rubbed it on my cock before lining its fat head against his hole. Slowly easing my way inside, I intended to take him carefully, not wanting to hurt him. Karl had other ideas though, because he rocked backward, impaling himself on my cock with that one fast move.

Gasping, I said, "Fuck, babe. Slow down! You're not an omega, your ass isn't made for this, remember?"

"My ass was made for your cock, and I wish for you to demonstrate it to me now," Karl rasped out in a low voice, already trying to rock back against me.

Pulling out briefly, I slammed my cock firmly back in with one furious thrust. Gripping the back of his neck with my right hand, I shoved his head down, pressing his face against the packed earth of the forest floor.

I held him there, working into a steady rhythm of slow retreats and then fast, hard plunges of my cock into that hungry channel. I released my angry frustration with each rapid thrust.

Fucking him hard and fast, I let my love shine through with each slow withdrawal. He bore back down on me through each hip pump, rocking his muscular ass onto my cock.

Reaching around with my left hand, I gripped his rock-hard dick. I jerked that meat in sync with my thrusts. The sound coming out of Karl's throat was something between a whimper and a groan.

I kept my grip tight on his neck as my pace increased. I fucked him hard and fast. Pounding into him, I channeled my fury into each thrust. He could take it, though. With each grunting rock of his hips, I knew that he was right there with me.

My balls tightened, and I knew I wouldn't last much longer. Karl came with a growl. His spurts of hot cum poured over my hand and onto the ground beneath him. The clenching of his ass created a vise-like grip that had me thrusting frantically, as I followed him over the edge into bliss.

I pushed in deeper, needing to be as far inside his body as I could get. My suddenly shaky legs began to collapse as I dropped down over him, pressing my chest against his back.

Sliding over his sweat-slicked skin, I grabbed his shoulders with trembling hands to anchor myself. I bit into his left shoulder with a growl, only to be rewarded by his answering groan of pleasured pain.

My vision starting to blur, I desperately fucked into him while gobs of cum shot out of my cock. I kept cumming, pouring so much of my nectar into his body, that I thought it might come out of his mouth.

We lay there like that for about ten minutes, or hours, who knew at that point. I didn't move until my softened cock slipped out, coming to rest in the welcoming curve of his cheeks. With a sated sigh, I rolled off to the side and snuggled up against him.

Karl turned, wrapping his strong arms around me and holding me close. We stayed there in each other's arms, my head resting on his fast-breathing chest. My nose filled with the musky odors of our mixed sweat and cum combined with the earthy aromas of the dirt we lay on and the pine trees around us, as I dozed off in my lover's embrace.

* * *

After a while, I woke up to the feel of Karl's hand stroking my hair.

"Ah, so now my poor, tired man has awakened, yes?"

"Hey, babe." I yawned, stretching back over the arm that was locked around my waist. "How long was I out? I'm sorry."

"Your body needed to rest, there is no reason to apologize. You were not asleep for longer than an hour."

"Yeah, but that's an hour that I could have spent with you."

"And you did, Owen. I enjoyed holding you and listening to your heart beat while you rested in my arms. This was a beautiful time for me, my love."

Lifting up, I leaned over and kissed his full lips. "Love you, babe. Today was good. I'm sorry I spazzed out earlier. About Zane?" I sighed, sitting up and pulling away to wrap my arms around my knees.

With a soft sigh, Karl sat up facing me with his arms resting across his knees. "I understand that you were unsettled by the way that Zane came upon us during a private moment. As I also know that you smelled him while he stood there watching us, just as I did. And yet, we kept kissing and providing him with a private show, yes?"

My suddenly flushed cheeks burned, as I avoided Karl's knowing gaze. I thought about it, and realized that yes, I had been aware of the man's presence the entire time. His sweet and spicy cookie scent mixed with that heady arousal would have been impossible to ignore.

"He does smell awfully sweet, right?" I said, looking up with a small smile.

"Yes, he certainly does."

"Karl, I'm happy with what we have together. I don't need an omega!"

"What if I do?"

"You saying that I'm not enough for you, Karl? Because it didn't seem that way a little while ago."

"Do not be like that, Owen. Please. I just want you to consider the idea of how our relationship could be enriched with the addition of the omega."

"Two's company, three's a crowd, Karl."

"Sometimes. Other times, three pieces create a whole."

"So, what are you suggesting? That the little twink is, I dunno, the missing side of our triangle?"

"Yes. That is exactly what I am suggesting."

"Karl. Babe. I'm still trying to wrap my brain around the two of us falling for each other. An inter-species relationship between two alphas is gonna be a hard enough sell for our friends and families. Now you want to form a menage?"

Karl sighed, then lifted a hand to rest on my arm. "Owen, can I ask you a question? You worry about other people's expectations and opinions. Yet, I want you to consider something. When do we shifters notice the scent of another shifter as anything more than pleasant or foul? When do we pick up on the nuances and put a flavor profile to their specific scent?"

My jaw dropped, as I jerked my head up to stare at him wide-eyed. Fuck. I'd never thought about what the fact of me knowing that Karl smelled like coconuts meant. To any other shifter, he would merely smell sweet. Only his fated-mate or parent would know what the exact scent entailed. And Zane's cookie scent? I never should have been able to pick up on that either! And, holy shit, what did it mean that Karl also recognized the scent?

He nodded slowly and smiled knowingly at me, correctly reading my mind as I suddenly realized what he had been suggesting.

"Now do you understand why I've asked you to give consideration to my attraction to Zane? If you would be honest, I would say our mutual attraction to him."

"Why are you so mellow about all this, Karl? I know that you're a laid back guy anyway, but you don't even seem surprised by this turn of events."

Karl bit his lip, his fair cheeks blushing slightly as he responded. "As you are aware, we bears are more sensitive to smells and pheromones than you wolves, yes?"

I nodded, thinking of how Doc Ollie always predicted pregnancies in our pack within a day of conception. He can smell the subtle change in hormones weeks before we wolves would be able to detect it.

"The day that Zane arrived here, I assisted the alpha who was driving the car with a flat tire. You remember Zane mentioning that moment?"

"Yeah, but that was what, over two years ago?"

"Yes. When I approached the car that day, the windows were down and I picked up his gingersnap scent before I ever reached the car."

"Seriously? And you didn't act on it? Why not?"

"It was not time. I was scenting his natural fragrance, but it was still emerging at the time. He was barely out of youth, and not ready for a mate yet. I knew that I would need to wait for him to finish maturing."

"Were we already together?"

"Yes. That is the other reason that I did not follow up on the young omega. I was already in love with you, enticed by your spicy cinnamon scent. I did not understand at the time what it meant, that I could recognize two scents, from two separate men. And the fact that you are both wolf shifters only made it that much more confusing for me."

"But still, Karl. You should have talked to me about it. I feel like you've had this big secret all this time, and I don't know how to feel about that."

"Please, Owen. Do not think that I have been keeping secrets from you. It was not like that, not intentionally anyway. It was more that I recognized him as a future mate, then filed it away and forgot about it until now."

"You expect me to believe that you've never thought about him at all since that day?"

"No, I do not expect that at all. I would be lying if I said that I had never wondered about him. At first, he came to mind from time to time, but then life moved on and I did not think about him anymore. I knew that he was meant to be our mate at some point, but there was no point in pining until that day comes. When fate decides it is time, then we will work things out. Of this, I have no doubt."

"But, why didn't you ever at least mention it to me? I could have been at least trying to prepare myself."

"Because you aren't meant to know these things until fate reveals it to you and you are able to catch your mate's scent. If I had told you earlier, you would not have believed me. It would also have made it awkward for you to be around him these past couple of years, would it not?"

"Well, you have a point there. I wouldn't have believed you if I couldn't smell it, I'll give you that. And we both know that I've never wanted to take on the responsibility of having an omega. Shit, I probably would've run for the hills."

"Exactly my point, my love. Now do you understand why I have kept this information to myself?"

"Yeah," I grudgingly replied. "But I still don't like it. I get it, but I don't like it."

"Which part bothers you, my love? Is it the fact that I kept my knowledge from you, or the fact that fate has given you an omega?"

"Fuck. I didn't even think about the part where I'm gonna have an omega. I was thinking about you keeping shit from me. What the hell am I gonna do with an omega, Karl? I'm not responsible like you. I wasn't cut out to be in a family. Hell, my own parents abandoned me as a pup."

"Owen. Just because you were left as a pup for the pack to raise does not mean that your family did not want you. Did you not tell me once that nobody in your pack knew where you had come from? That you had been found in the woods as a pup?"

"Yeah. And no one ever stepped forward to claim me, so who knows where I came from originally."

"I have thought about this situation, and I cannot help but wonder if your parents were not perhaps victims of an accident, or even if you had been taken from them and possibly left behind when your abductors were shocked because you had shifted into a pup, yes? Stranger things have occurred. While we may never know where you came from originally, even you cannot deny the strong bonds of friendship that you have with your Alpha and the other men in your circle of friends. You cannot say that you are not cut out for family life; you have made a family of your pack, and you have been perfectly faithful to me."

"Dude. Of course, I'm faithful to you. I wouldn't feel right even imagining being with another man now."

"Perhaps. Close your eyes, my love. Picture Zane. Can you imagine how soft his skin would feel under our rough tongues as we lick it together? Think of his sweet smell. Imagine watching him flush so prettily, while you watch him take my knot? Now, imagine those sweet pink lips wrapped around your cock. Are you able to imagine all that, Owen? Do not lie to me now, your body is already betraying you, my love."

I narrowed my eyes at him, seeing how hungrily he was looking at my now hard cock. Fuuuck. I had been sucked in by the low, soothing voice describing that scenario with Zane, and it had seriously turned me on.

"My eyes are up here, Karl. No looking at the merchandise unless you plan to take care of the situation that you caused."

"The situation being your hard cock?"

"Exactly."

He eagerly pushed my arms out of the way and spread my knees, pushing his way in between them to get at my cock.

"I have one stipulation, Owen, before I swallow your seed."

Gulping at that, I nodded silently.

"I want you to close your eyes and pretend that my lips are Zane's lips. My tongue is his tongue. My hands," he fondled my balls and leered up at me. "My hands are Zane's hands. If you cannot picture him at all while I give you pleasure, then I will drop the idea of a trio altogether. But remember, I will know if you are lying to me, my love."

Rolling my eyes, I cursed our shifter sniffers that kept us from being able to lie convincingly. "Alright. I'll try. But will you be pissed if I can't? I don't want to keep you from your fated-mate."

"*Our* fated-mate, Owen. That is why I can take this risk. Because I already know that you would have been picturing him anyway. Now that you have smelled his delightful scent, you will be unable to resist thinking of him. Fate is bringing him into your life now. Yours and mine. You will see."

Leaning back on my hands, I pushed my cock towards his face. "Alright, babe. Prove to me that I'm able to picture another man. Do your worst."

The last thing I saw as I closed my eyes was the gleam in Karl's eyes as he swallowed my cock in one quick move. Rolling my head back, I enjoyed the feel of my man licking, sucking, and fucking my cock with his mouth, while his nimble fingers toyed with my balls and teased my hole.

I relaxed into the fantastic blow-job, and damned if I wasn't picturing *pushing my cock into Zane's mouth, while his freckled little face flushed pink. His pale green eyes watered when he almost choked from the girth of my fat cock pushing its way into his throat.*

He would pull back, strings of drool connecting his mouth to the fat head of my cock while he gasped for air. Once I knew he was okay, I would firmly grasp the back of his carrot red head and push him back down on my cock.

I could feel the heat of his mouth, the swirl of his small pink tongue as he drilled the tip of it into my leaking slip, and my balls would be tightening up as I began to—

"Nnngggghhh!" I groaned as my stomach tightened and spurts of cum shot into the back of Za—er, Karl's throat. Opening my eyes, I found him watching me through hooded eyes as he eagerly swallowed my entire load.

I fell back on the ground, completely depleted, as Karl flopped down next to me and leaned over for a kiss. Resting his hand on my chest, he smiled at me and said, "Now tell me, my love. Who was the man in your mind while you were receiving the pleasure of my mouth?"

Groaning, I said, "You know damned well that I was picturing Zane. You were right, Karl. Where before I never would have been able to imagine another man touching me, it was natural to imagine the omega taking my cock into his pretty mouth. You must be psychic to already know the answer, babe."

"That is one possibility. The other is that you were moaning his name while I was sucking you down."

"Seriously?"

Karl smiled gently, and softly kissed my cheek. "Seriously, my love. We will need to make a decision soon, and decide when to speak with your Alpha."

"What? Why now? I mean, do we really have to rush into things?"

"Owen, I have all the patience in the world. However, I have a feeling that the way fate is already intervening, that things will be sped up by force if we do not come to a solution on our own."

"What do you mean? You don't think that Zane will out us, do you?"

"No, nor would I care. My concern is that our mate hasn't

had his first heat yet, and I can smell that it is close. If we don't decide things before it comes, then we might find ourselves in an untenable position."

"Like what?"

"Well, for instance, there are unmated alphas in your pack. Any of them would be unable to resist an omega's heat, if he has no alpha already there to stake a claim."

I growled in the back of my throat.

"Exactly, my love. Your wolf would never accept that, nor would my bear. The other situation is if you are forced to claim him alone, without me present."

"No. I couldn't do that. It wouldn't feel right without you there."

"Then we have but one solution, my love. We must approach your Alpha as soon as possible. If your pack is unwilling to accept us, we will petition the Alpha of my den."

"Jake will accept us. I know that in my heart. It's just my head that worries, you know?"

"I understand, my love. Shall we head to your lodge then? I did not wish to rush things, but my bear is feeling an urgency that is compelling me to do this now."

I grinned with complete understanding, because as we'd been talking, my wolf had been pacing frantically beneath the surface.

"Then let's go talk to Jake, babe. No time like the present, right?"

"That was my point, yes."

We exchanged one last kiss as a single couple, and shifted into our animal counterparts. It was time to go see about claiming our omega, whether my human side was ready or not.

"You seriously mean that you believe yourself to be mated with a bear?" Jake said to Owen, shock clearly written across his face. "And another alpha? Not an omega?"

We were seated in the Alpha's office having a private conversation. I was trying to stay out of it, for now, while my mate spoke to his Alpha. I knew that he would afford me the same courtesy if the situation were reversed.

"Actually," Owen answered. "That's kind of why we're here. This is a weird situation, and I don't know that I've heard of anything like it before. But Karl and I are both fated to an omega."

The Alpha's eyes flicked over to give me an appraising look, before going back to rest on his friend. "If you're each fated to an omega, then why are we even having this conversation? Obviously you can't be fated to your omega and mate each other, your animal halves would never accept it."

Owen looked at me, at a loss as to how to continue.

"If I may speak, Alpha?" I said courteously.

"Of course, Karl. We're all friends here, go ahead."

"Thank you. What Owen is trying, and failing, to explain is that he and I are fated-mates, both fated equally to the same omega. The reason we are here is to get your blessing, because this is an unusual situation."

"Wait, what now?" Alpha looked shocked by my statement, but not at all upset or disgusted. "How is that possible?"

"We do not know this ourselves, Alpha. But Owen and I are not only able to smell each other's true scents, we are also both able to smell the true scent of one of your pack omegas."

"Oh. Okay. That makes sense then." Jake flashed a relieved grin at Owen before looking back at me. "I was afraid that you guys were trying to tell me that you were taking Owen away from our pack. Not gonna lie, I was kinda freaking out about that."

"Seriously?" Owen asked. "You don't care about the whole trio thing, or me and a freakin' bear mating Zane? You were actually scared that I was gonna leave? Wow! I didn't realize I was that important to you."

"Of course, Owen. Come on, how long have we been friends? You've always been there for me, why wouldn't I be there for you? Wait." He stopped, his mouth dropping open. "Did you say that Zane is your omega?"

Owen blushed, looking down at his feet while he nodded.

Alpha laughed and shook his head. "Wow, that's gonna be fun to watch. That kid is sweet as can be, but damn, he has got walls protecting his walls, if you know what I mean."

Curious and immediately concerned, I said, "Zane has been hurt? What are these walls of which you speak?"

Alpha's kind eyes lit on me as he replied, "Do you know anything about Zane, Karl? Has Owen told you his story?"

"Um, I don't really know his story, Jake," Owen said quietly, "I've pretty much been ignoring him and the other guys that I don't know. I've been a little preoccupied with Karl here for the past couple of years."

Alpha looked hurt when Owen told him how long we had been together. "Owen, seriously? I thought this was new! Do you mean to tell me that you've been together that long, and you didn't even tell your best friends? Shit, dude. I thought we were closer than that. Did you even tell Daniel?"

Shaking his head, Owen said: "No, I haven't told anyone.

I wasn't sure how anyone would react when I told them that I wanted to mate another alpha, and that I was in a mixed relationship with a bear."

"I'm going to forgive you for underestimating us, Owen, because I know how you worry about losing people. Here's the deal. You know my Aunt Kat?"

Turning to me, Alpha explained that his aunt was the one who owned this lodge and had welcomed them all to live here when they had formed their pack.

"What about Aunt Kat?" Owen asked.

Jake smiled, his eyes looking off in the distance as if reliving happy, old memories. "Aunt Kat was mated to my Uncle Julio. He died a few years before we settled here, but he was an awesome cat."

Looking at Owen, making sure he had his attention, Jake continued, "I mean that literally, as in he was a Jaguar shifter. My family has no problem with mixed relationships. Love is love, right? Besides, who are we to question Fenris and the mate, or in your case mates, that he has chosen to give you?"

Owen looked shocked, and I smiled, happy to know that this Alpha was as fair-minded a man as I had always assumed him to be.

"When we settled here and formed this pack, my Aunt Kat had just one request for me. She wanted *all* shifters to be welcome here, particularly those in mixed relationships. I had no problem agreeing to that request because I feel the same way. People who have a problem with it wouldn't belong in our pack anyway. It's written into our pack by-laws, in fact. I wanted to make sure that the rule will stand when I'm no longer here, you know?"

"Owen, I do hate to say that I told you so," I said with a loving smile. "But I believe that I have been telling you for some time now that your pack would accept our relationship."

"Yeah, I mean, it's definitely different," Alpha said, with a grin to Owen. "But then, who am I to judge? You guys just do you. The pack will support you. So, why isn't Zane sitting in on this meeting?"

"Ah, yes, Zane," I said. "He is not yet aware of our desire to claim him. We wanted to speak to you first, to make certain how you and the pack would feel if we should go forward. But first, may I ask what you meant about these walls and the background of our mate?"

Alpha sighed softly, a sad look on his face. "Zane was the younger brother of my old friend, Tommy Collins. Do you remember him, Owen?"

At Owen's nod, Alpha explained to me, "Tommy was our friend Micah's best friend from our old pack. We played together as pups. Owen's and my best friend, Daniel, is Micah's cousin."

I nodded slowly, my brain carefully filing away these familial relationships that the Alpha was detailing for me.

"Anyway," he continued, "Tommy and his parents were killed in a car wreck on the way to Zane's high school graduation. After that, he had to watch his family home be sold, because omegas weren't allowed to own property in our old pack. His only living relative was his cousin, a nasty little bastard named Steve."

Owen looked up then, "Seriously? Zane had to deal with that fucker? No wonder the kid is so damned snarky."

Alpha grinned and continued his story. "Steve did sell the house and put the money in an account for Zane. So, at least he did get his money before he came here. But he lived with Steve for the entire year between his parent's death and when Micah brought him here. From what I understand, Steve was using him as free childcare for his four pups."

"That's bullshit, and yet, not at all surprising," Owen said, with a dark look on his face. "Steve would be one to take advantage of an omega's nurturing skills. I see Zane with the pups around here a lot. Apparently, he likes pups?"

Alpha nodded. "Oh, yeah. Zane is great with the pups, they friggin' love him. Zane tends to be introverted, I've noticed. He's friendly enough with the pack, but he hasn't really gotten tight with anyone here, except for the pups. They're the only ones that he lets his walls down around."

"It sounds as if you have given this some thought, Alpha. Have you had reason to be concerned for our Zane?" I asked, getting concerned myself now. It was not good for an omega not to have ties with his pack. Omegas needed family, it was just how they were wired.

"No, not really," Alpha said. "My mate, Kai, tends to worry over the various pack members from time to time, and I get to hear him fuss about it privately when he gets worried. He has been watching Zane, because he wants him to have friends. His routine of taking long nature walks by himself, or shutting himself in the dorm to read or sleep, are like red flags to Kai."

"Maybe he's just shy, or an introvert," Owen said. "Nothing wrong with that. Still. I'm gonna have to talk to him. Is it okay if Karl goes up to the dorms with me, so we can go find him?"

"I don't care. You two are mates, go wherever you want. Just don't pop a knot where any of the pups can wander in and see you, that's the only thing I give a shit about. Is there a special rush on this, or are you just anxious to claim him now?"

Owen grinned at his buddy, shaking his head. "Well, my wolf is pacing, and so is Karl's bear. Karl says that Zane may go into his first heat anytime now, and we don't want our omega to be unclaimed and tempt any of our pack alphas. It would be awkward when the pheromones passed and I had to kill them for touching my mate, you know?"

I added my thoughts. "We would also like for Zane to accept us while in his own mind, not when he is lost to the hormonal influence of his heat cycle. It would not be acceptable for us to claim him without prior consent. We wish to court him, while it is still possible, yes?"

"Well then. I guess this is where I wish you both good luck. Zane's a tough nut, so you'll need it, if you ask me."

"Shut up, Jake," Owen said with a grin. "Like you know about omegas. You got lucky with the first one that fell into your lap, admit it."

"Trust me, Kai will never let me forget that! But seriously, if you guys are worried about time, then go ahead and track him down. I don't want to tie you up when you have an omega to convince that your fugly ass is fated for him. Now, he might like Karl. He's always seemed cool, but you? Shit. I feel bad for the guy already."

I started to get irritated at the slight to my alpha mate, but quickly realized that the Alpha was teasing when Owen started laughing. When we rose to leave, they exchanged a fist bump and then the Alpha reached out to shake my hand.

* * *

As Owen led me up to the dormitories on the third floor, I looked around at the beautiful lodge. I had helped to patrol the borders of their territory for the past few years as a favor to my friend, Doc, but I had never been inside. It was a beautiful home.

I envied the wolves and their pack mentality. It must be nice to always have many friends and family around to support you. We bears were loners by nature. It was not common for bears to have large families, or to retain close ties to their birth family once mated. Aside from holiday functions, we rarely interacted.

In fact, I had not seen my twin brother, Kane, in four years. He met his mate, Ivy, and they went off to live deep in the woods of her den territory. I missed my brother, so very much, but he never returned my texts or calls. I was grateful that my mates are wolves, perhaps now I would have the closeness of family.

Owen took my hand as we climbed the stairs to the third floor where he lived. I had spent many nights alone in my bed, wondering what my love's home was like. What he saw when first opening his eyes in the morning or who he sat with during mealtimes. To finally be getting a peek into his private life was a dream come true for a lonely bear like me.

Stopping in front of an open doorway, Owen squeezed my hand, as if seeking support. We walked in, and there he lay on a single bunk near a window that overlooked the woods surrounding the lodge. Alone, our Zane was reading a book in the fading light of the afternoon sun that filtered through the glass.

Zane glanced up at our approach, fumbling and dropping his book when he realized who had entered his private quarters. He sat up on the edge of his bed, hanging his legs over the side, and crossing his arms across his chest.

"Hey, um, you guys aren't supposed to be in here," he said nervously.

"It's cool, Gingersnaps. We cleared it with Alpha already."

His lips pursed together, nearly disappearing as he scowled. "And why exactly did you need to do that? Didn't you get to berate me enough in the woods earlier? What, you had to chase me down to dish out more insults? Honestly, Owen. I said that I wouldn't say anything about you guys, and I won't. Like I even care what you do in private. Geez."

Releasing Owen's hand, I stepped over and knelt down in front of him. "That is not why we are here, Zane. In fact, I believe that Owen's intent was to apologize for his earlier behavior."

Turning my head to look up at Owen, I flashed him a warning look. He sighed and motioned to the bed beside our omega.

"Can I sit down? Is that cool?"

Zane looked horrified, but nodded his consent. Owen sat

down beside him, close enough to put him on edge yet far enough to feign innocence.

"Look. I was a real dick earlier. I'm sorry. I shouldn't have freaked you out like that, or chased you."

Zane looked at him curiously, his eyes flickering over to me for a moment before turning back to Owen. Finally, he nodded.

"I'm sorry too. I shouldn't have watched you guys like a pervy stalker. You had a right to be pissed."

"Maybe, but I didn't have to take it to the level I did. So, are we cool?"

Zane nodded with a shy smile. "Yes, we're cool. But I don't understand. Why did you guys come up here just to apologize? I mean, I appreciate it and all. I'm just confused I think? It's like you tracked me down or something."

Reaching a hand over to cup his knee, I looked into his pale, moss green eyes and said, "We did track you down, Zane. We need to talk to you, if you do not mind?"

"What about? I already said that we're cool now."

Shaking my head, I said, "No, not about that. We need to discuss being mates with you."

"Why do you need to discuss the fact that you're mates with me?"

"Because," Owen said gruffly. "You are also our mate. We

need to figure out what that means, preferably before you go into heat or something."

Zane looked from me to Owen, and then back at me again. Before he could do more than gape, his eyes rolled back in his head and he collapsed sideways into Owen's lap. Zane had fainted.

CHAPTER 4

ZANE

"You wanna run that by me again? I asked Karl, from my perch on his lap. I had passed out, waking up to find myself cradled in the bear's large arms. I could think of worse places to be. But dear Fenris, how embarrassing to faint in front of not just one, but two of the sexiest alphas I'd ever known.

"Zane. Tell me what I smell like to you, sweetest."

"Coconuts," I answered without hesitation.

"And Owen? How does he smell?"

I glanced at the other alpha, casually sitting beside Karl while he listened intently to our conversation. Looking back at Karl, I said softly, "Owen smells like cinnamon sticks."

"Exactly right. Did you notice this morning that Owen

and I were both able to correctly detect your exact scent profile?"

I nodded, unsure if I liked where this conversation was going.

"When you were in school, did your instructors talk about fated-mates? And the ways in which they find each other?"

"Well, yeah. Of course. There's the immediate attraction, naturally. The jolt of awareness when you touch each other," I paused with a shiver. A flare of electricity had ran up my body right then, as Owen had lifted my legs and stretched them across his lap.

Shuddering, I looked back at Karl. "And most important, is the fact that only true-mates can—" I froze, suddenly realizing Karl's point.

"Yes, only truly fated-mates can recognize the true scent of one another." Karl finished for me. "To the rest of your pack, you likely smell like a spicy-sweet combination. Owen would smell spicy, and I would smell sweet."

I looked into Karl's grayish-green eyes, noting for the first time the streaks of copper that flared out around his pupils. They were amazing eyes; I could gaze into their striated beauty for hours and still not feel as if I'd seen their true depths. I jolted when I saw my hand cupping his tanned cheek, unsure of when my hand had moved there without my knowledge.

Turning, Karl pressed a kiss into my palm. I gasped at the sensual spark that shot straight from my palm to my dick from that chaste kiss. A deep dimple flashed in his right cheek when Karl smiled as he leaned forward to claim my lips next.

It was my first kiss. It was a fantastic kiss. It was a kiss that was everything, soft and tender all at once, just like I'd always imagined that a kiss should be. His lips pressed gently against mine, head tilting slightly to get a better angle. Before I could process what was happening, a tongue thrust out to lick along the curve of my top lip.

I gasped, and when my lips parted, his tongue came all the way into my mouth and tentatively stroked my tongue. My hands went around his neck as his arms went around my waist to pull me closer to his chest. I heard a soft moan, and pulled away to see Owen watching us hungrily.

Not certain how I felt about this, but strangely aroused at the same time, I nestled my cheek beneath Karl's chin. I watched Owen silently, moving my hand out tentatively to reach out to him. He took my hand, pressing it between his palms, and smiled shyly at me.

"You can feel it, the pull between us, yes?"

"I-I think so," I stammered. "But I don't know what to do. I've never felt anything like this before."

"Like what, sweetest? The magnetism between the three of us?"

I nodded slowly. "Yes. But how is it possible?"

"That we do not know ourselves. It is a mystery, is it not? I have not seen such a relationship before, but that does not mean that others do not exist."

Owen stroked my hand, appearing deep in thought. "Jake said it best, I think. He said that love is love, and if Fenris has blessed us with a mate or mates, then who are we to question it, you know?"

"But what about the fact that Karl is a bear? He didn't have a problem with that either?"

"Nope. He was more concerned that you and Karl would pull me away from the pack. You know that he's been my best friend since we were pups, right?"

I smiled sadly. "Yeah, I don't know that I remember you, but I definitely remember Micah, Jake, and Daniel hanging out with my brother."

"I don't remember you either, to be honest. I totally remember Tommy, but I didn't hang out with him until I was given a new foster mom. Daniel's mom was my foster mom's sister. That's how I met Micah and Jake, through Daniel. He included me with his friends, and we all hung out at school. I wasn't allowed to hang out after school, because I had chores. That's probably why we didn't meet back then."

"Plus, I was six years younger than Tommy. That's another reason that I didn't meet you back then. The guys let me follow them around, but not as much when they hit their teen years. And once I was designated omega, Tommy never let me around his friends. What about your family? Do you have a brother?"

"Owen does not have blood relatives, sweetest. Your pack is his family."

I looked into Owen's lonely gaze, and finally felt a spark of kinship. "Well, that's something that we have in common then, isn't it? I may not know what it felt like to grow up without a family, but I definitely know what it feels like to be alone in the world now."

Owen winked at me and immediately lightened the mood. "What about your dear cousin, Steve? He counts as family."

Fighting a giggle, I said, "Well, if you claim me as a mate, then my family is your family. I guess that means we'll have to invite Steve and his family up for Winter Solstice then? I mean, since he is family after all. You'll particularly love his pups. They have no rules or boundaries. Their mom believes that putting limits on pups keeps them from learning to expand their minds."

Karl's sudden booming laugh should have scared me, but instead it warmed me. Owen pretended to scowl at Karl, which only had him laughing that much harder.

"Gee," I said, "I didn't think it was that funny."

"No, the reason that Karl is laughing his ass off is because he knows that I get uncomfortable around pups."

I sucked in a breath. "Really? But, umm, what if..." I let my voice trail off, too shy to complete my thought.

Owen took a deep breath, and said, "Karl says that it will be different with my own pups. It's not that I don't like them, not really. I've just never really had experience with pups, or with being part of a regular family like that."

He squeezed my hand, and looked at me earnestly. "I'm not going to let that keep you or Karl from having pups. I want to want them, if that makes sense? I'm just, umm, nervous."

My heart melted as I watched the cocky alpha open up to me like that. I had no idea how this was supposed to work, but I knew in that moment that I was all in. We would just have to figure it out together.

"Now that we have spent a bit of time together, perhaps we shall decide our next move?"

I nodded at Karl's words. "Yeah, we really can't hang out here in the omega dorms much longer. I mean, only Luke and Ryan live up here with me right now, but we're still not supposed to have alphas in here."

Owen quirked a brow. "I didn't realize that you guys had rules like that."

"It's Kai's rule. He wanted the omegas to have a safe

place, where we wouldn't have to be around alphas if we didn't want to be."

"Is that why you stay in here so much?" Owen asked with a concerned look on his face. "I hope that we've never made you feel uncomfortable."

"No," I answered quickly. "Not at all. I don't mind any of the pack alphas, everyone in the pack is nice. I guess, I just like to be alone?"

"That sounds more like a bear trait, than that of a wolf," Karl commented.

"Yeah, I guess it kinda does, right?" I giggled. "Seriously though, I got in the habit after my family died and I was living with my cousin. It was a crazy household, and I lived in a room over the garage. Whenever I had time, I went there to decompress. Sometimes it's easier to be alone than to try and deal with a noisy crowd of people, you know?"

Karl said, "I know of many bears who would agree with you."

"But you don't?"

"Personally? No, I do not. I tire of being alone. I have long cherished the dream of having family of my own."

"And you, Owen?"

"I'm kinda in the middle. I like being with my friends, but

I also like having down time. That's how I met Karl, when I was hanging out in the woods."

"Oh? What, on patrol duty?"

"No, I like to go camping. There's a spot near the waterfalls a little north of here that is perfect. Not a soul for miles, and fresh water, what more could a guy want, you know?"

"That sounds awesome," I said enviously.

Owen looked a little surprised. "You would be into that? When we go, we stay up there for days, sometimes a week or more."

"We? You and Karl go?"

I wasn't jealous. It was more like, I was late to the party. Like, they had all these shared experiences and private jokes, and I wasn't sure how I'd fit into their world.

"Yeah, Karl's the one who introduced me to the spot. We've had some great times up there, haven't we, babe?"

Karl shook his head, chuckling under his breath. "Owen, my love. You need to show a little more sensitivity."

"What did I say?"

"It was nothing you said, Owen. I am just thinking that perhaps Zane may feel a little left out when you speak of our shared history."

I pulled my feet free of Owen's lap, and scrambled free of

Karl's embrace. I stood up and took a step back, saying, "It's okay. I get it. You guys are always going to be a couple first, right?"

Karl stood and put his hands on my shoulders, ducking his head to make eye contact. "Zane. Please, sweetest, do not do this to yourself. Remember that this is also new for us. We will need to learn how to be together. I am sorry that our shared history will make you feel as though you are a third wheel. That is not our intent. Owen and I want to love you equally, the way that true-mates should, yes?"

Owen groaned and threw himself backward on my bed, laying there with his arm over his eyes. "Seriously? That's what got your panties in a twist? I totally didn't mean it like that. I was actually about to ask you if you'd like to go up there with us for a few days. We could go camping, and it would be a great way to get to know each other better without our gossipy friends watching our every move."

I stiffened, ducking out of Karl's hold. Stalking across the room to calm myself, I shoved a hand through my hair and snapped, "You want me to go into the dang woods with you, and you lead with a put-down?"

Owen sat up, looking at me quizzically. "Put-down? For fuck's sake? What did I say now?"

"Well, if you don't know, I'm not going to tell you," I said, shifting my weight onto one hip and crossing my arms over my chest.

Karl gave a low growl, and shocked me when he spoke with a hint of irritation, something rarely seen in a bear. "Enough! We cannot hope to make this work if the two of you act like children. Owen, you need to choose your words and consider Zane's feelings before you speak. Zane, you need to give Owen a break too. He was not raised by loving parents as you were, and he does not often think before he speaks."

I lowered my arms, but still spoke stiffly. "And how is this my problem? I'm not the one who came to either of your rooms with another alpha in tow, acting all sweet and spouting talk of happy matings between three people. Maybe this is too crazy to work. If Owen and I can't even be civil for twenty minutes, how are we supposed to build a life together?"

Something about my words must have sparked something in Owen, because he got up and slowly walked toward me. I had a hard time focusing on his face' I was torn between admiring his long legs and the promising bulge that filled the crotch of his faded jeans.

Stopping in front of me, Owen gave me a surprisingly shy smile, and reached for my hands. Threading his fingers through mine, he spoke softly but earnestly. "You're right. I lost sight of the fact that our mating with you is the beginning of the three of us building a life together. Karl's right, I suck at thinking before I speak. But for the first time in my life, I want to try. Can I start by saying that I'm sorry for being a fucking idiot?"

I blushed, and nodded my head. "I'm sorry too. I get pissed super quick. I should wait and see what you're actually meaning to say, instead of just finding fault with the first thing that pops out of your mouth."

"I know I told you that I'm scared to have pups. But I'm not scared to start a future with you. Fenris wouldn't have put us together if we didn't fit. I have to believe that, especially after seeing so many of our friends find fulfillment with their true-mates. Can you be patient with me, while I learn how to be a good mate to you?"

Before I could answer, Karl spoke from over Owen's shoulder. "This is a good start, but first there is a more important question that we need to ask. Zane, are you willing to let us claim you for our omega? Will you allow us to love you, and make you our mate, sweetest?"

Biting my lip, I nodded quickly. "Y-y-yes. I-I want th-th-that." Shaking my head, I took a breath and fought my stutter. "I want that with both of you, because Owen is right. Fenris wouldn't have brought us together if we didn't fit."

Looking up at Owen, I smiled nervously. "I'll try to be more patient with you, while you try to work on your words. I'm sorry I turn into a drama queen from like, zero to sixty. We can learn to be good mates together, okay?"

"I like the sound of that, baby. Together has a good ring, doesn't it?"

I stood on tip-toes, and placed a hesitant kiss on his mouth. Owen's lips were slightly rougher than Karl's, but no less intense. Karl's kiss had been soft and tender, while Owen kissed with a fire that spoke of banked passion waiting to be ignited. I felt a large arm come around my back, and then Karl's lips brushed against the side of my neck.

I moaned and broke the kiss, staring up into Owen's eyes while Karl nuzzled and kissed my omega gland at the curve of my neck and shoulder. My body was shuddering, visibly shaking with desire for these two men. Karl's head came up, and he stood there in place while giving me one long sniff.

Looking at him curiously, I said, "Dude, is this sniffing people fetish a bear thing? Cuz we wolves don't go around just obviously sniffing each other all the time. No offense, it just makes me paranoid, like maybe I stink or something."

Karl grinned, and said with a twinkle in his eye, "No, I do not have a fetish for sniffing people. I was concerned that the power of our combined alpha pheromones might affect your hormone levels. I was attempting to discreetly check those levels."

I stared up at him, totally stunned. "First of all, eww. You can smell my hormone levels? Seriously? I'm not sure if that's a personal violation, or just weird, but I'll get back to you on that one. Secondly, you're checking to see if I'm about to go into heat? Because that's what I was picking up between the lines there. And that's just, like, totally gross!"

Karl looked like he was at a loss for words, while Owen grinned and rolled his eyes at me conspiratorially.

"Don't mind, Karl. He doesn't mean to invade our personal space. And yeah, it's totally a bear thing. But it does come in handy, trust me on that."

I was still embarrassed, and said in a mumbled whisper, *"But he was checking me for signs of heat, Owen! I've never even, umm, actually had that happen yet."*

Poor Karl looked mortified to have embarrassed me, while Owen was still grinning like it was the funniest thing ever. Still, he surprised me by patiently explaining Karl's motives.

"Sorry you're embarrassed, baby. You know that wasn't Karl's intent. And once we've been mated, things like this won't be embarrassing at all. It's just nature, right? But I get it. Especially if it's never happened to you before. We just don't want you to choose us because your heat is pushing you. We want you to make the decision freely."

I chewed my lip, listening to his words thoughtfully. After a moment, I turned and threw my arms around Karl's waist, pressing my cheek against his wide chest.

"It's okay, Karl. I won't be embarrassed anymore, if you won't either, okay? Owen's right. It's nature, and it sucks. But, I'm glad that you care enough to want to know that I chose you with my brain, not my d-d-dick."

I totally blushed as I stuttered over the word dick, to Owen's delight. He was laughing so hard that after a few seconds, Karl and I were laughing too.

"Holy fuck," Owen said after he caught his breath. "Karl, he can't even say the word dick without blushing. We're so screwed, this guy is gonna kill us with his sweetness."

Karl smiled indulgently, leaning down to kiss my temple as my eyes flashed with irritation at Owen. "Remember, Zane. You have promised to be more patient with our idiot mate and his careless words."

Looking over at Owen, he said, "And yes, I am aware of this sweetness. That is why I have decided to name him that. He is my sweetness."

"Seriously? Then, what is Owen?" I asked curiously, knowing full good and well that I was far from sweet.

"Owen is simply my love. Although, you will both own my heart, sweetness."

I could melt at this big bear. Seriously, I totally could.

"So, I never got an answer earlier, or maybe I never got around to asking. But anyway, what do you guys think about the three of us going up to the falls and camping where we can work our shit out privately?"

Karl looked at me questioningly after Owen's request, while Owen bounced on the balls of his feet like one of the pups I baby-sat. Rolling my eyes, I grinned and said, "Sure, let me pack a bag."

"Take only what you can carry, Gingersnap. Karl and I are gonna be loaded down with tents, food, equipment, and shit. And we have to hike up there, the road only goes so far."

"Dude. I've totally been camping before, I'm not allergic to being outside. Hello, you saw me walking through the woods just this morning. I had an older brother, remember? Our dad used to take us camping, fishing, and hunting every chance he got."

Karl spoke before Owen could answer. "That sounds great, sweetness. Why don't you let me help you pack, while Owen goes down to the kitchen and sees if there's food we can take or if we need to stop by the country store on our way up the mountain."

"We're not going through our woods?"

"No, sweetness. We will drive most of the way there, and then it will be a couple hours hike from the parking area."

Excited about the idea, I gave Karl a quick kiss on the cheek. After I gave Owen a matching one, I grabbed my old backpack and started filling it up. I heard Owen leaving the room, and glanced over to see Karl sitting on the bed. I thought for a second, then took a deep breath for courage. Walking over to the bed, I swung a leg over his lap. I sat down, straddling his legs, so that I could look him in the face while we talked..

"Can I talk to you for a minute?"

"Of course, Zane." He smiled, brushing a hand through my hair. "I am yours, always. What is it that you wish to speak of, sweetness?"

"Umm, I was wondering if I should just pack my suitcase with the rest of my stuff really quick, so that it will be easy to grab when we get back. We can leave it on Owen's bed or something. I know that Luke would love to have this bed by the window, and we both know that I won't be living in this room ever again. I mean, we'll all be mated when we return, won't we?"

I blushed, ducking my head to play with one of the brass buttons on his plaid shirt.

Resting his hands on my hips, Karl pressed a soft kiss to my forehead. "Yes, I believe that will be the case. Will you allow me to help you? I believe this is a good plan."

Tucking my hands between our chests, I curled up against him, snuggling into the heat of his body. His coconut smell got more intense all of a sudden, and I felt a hard erection pushing against my belly, where I was pressed against his larger body. I was intrigued by it, but at the same time, it didn't feel right to explore things without Owen present.

"Umm, we should probably get that packing done, huh?"

Karl chuckled. "Yes, sweetness. Let us pack your suit-cases, so that we can go join our missing mate."

* * *

An hour later, we were riding in Karl's fully packed SUV, heading for the mountain where we would be camping. My bags were waiting on Owen's bed, to be moved wher-ever we decided to settle in when we returned.

Our friends, Micah and Daniel, had both been a little weirded out when they saw my alpha mates loading the car and heard our news. Micah was more than a little protective of me, and he had pulled me away by the elbow to talk to me. My mates had both looked like they were ready to do battle when they saw that, but I waved them off. They hadn't looked happy, but they had let me go talk to him without interrupting.

"Zane," Micah had said. "Is this what you really want? Both of them? I mean, I can see you and Owen, but Karl too?"

"Micah, Owen and I are both hot-headed redheads. Do you think that we could manage to be together without killing each other? Seriously?"

He had grinned at that one.

"Besides, Micah. All three of us are fated-mates. We can smell each other's true scents, and we feel that pull. I didn't wake up this morning and choose for this to happen, it was dropped into my life by Fenris' will. Would you deny me the same happiness that you share with Aries?"

"No. I'm sorry to second guess you, Zany. I just feel like I owe it to Tommy to at least ask, okay?"

I smiled at the familiar childhood nickname. "Okay, Micah. Now, because you're being so cool, I'll do you a solid."

He raised a brow, and grinned when I said, "You get to drop this bombshell on Aries and his friends. Kai might know from Jake already, but he also might not. So, you might wanna get on that if you want to be the first with the news. I mean, this is kinda juicy gossip, right? If I remember right, the guys are all up at the creek with the pups this afternoon, so they probably don't know yet."

We had wandered back over to the car then, where Micah gave me a long hug. Owen said his own good-byes to Daniel, and we hit the road soon after. I was tucked into the only free corner of the back seat, while the alphas rode up together in front.

This was my suggestion, since they both had much longer legs and larger bodies than I did. Plus, it gave me a little alone time to catch my breath before things progressed. I was excited, nervous, and and slightly scared. Yeah, this was going to be an interesting night.

CHAPTER 5

OWEN

"You okay there, *Zany*?" I asked with a grin, knowing that he was about to get pissed, probably. I was quickly getting addicted to watching that pale skin pink up under all those cute little freckles. Anytime Zane got pissed, excited, embarrassed, whatever, he blushed. I fucking loved it.

"Don't call me that, Owen! Micah only gets away with it because he knew me when I was five and my brother called me that."

"So what? Now nobody else can call you that unless they dare risk the ire of the fierce little gingersnaps?"

"Owen."

"Zane."

Karl rolled his eyes us, but was staying out of it. He knew that Zane and I needed to find our own equilibrium.

"Seriously though, Zane. It's kinda steep for this last quarter mile. Do you need to stop and rest?"

"Because I'm a weak little omega without your big alpha muscles?"

Karl snorted, but I carefully replied, "No, gingersnaps. Because you aren't used to hiking at this altitude like we are. The first couple times I came, I almost wanted a break myself. I'm actually being thoughtful, try not to be too shocked."

Zane was quiet for moment, then he said quietly, "Would it up screw our timing if we stopped for a few minutes?"

Without a word, Karl and I stopped right there. We both dropped the heavy bags that we were carrying, and made a show of stretching our muscles. We totally could have made it the rest of the way without a problem, but we wanted to make sure that Zane was okay.

Zane seemed pretty strong, but he wasn't used to the terrain like we were. I hadn't been lying when I'd said that. Zane watched us, then quickly shrugged out of his own backpack and went over to sit in the shade of a large redwood tree. Without hesitation, Karl and I went over and dropped down to sit on either side of our smaller mate.

"Sorry if I'm screwing up our schedule. My calves are burning, and I just wanted a short break. We can go whenever you guys want."

I glanced over at Zane's flushed face. He really had needed this break.

"It's cool. I'm glad you took me at my word and asked for a break. Shit, I'm glad to have a chance to set all that crap down and take a break myself."

Karl looked over at me with a knowing smirk. I shrugged, and grinned back at him. I figured that if I wanted to be a good mate to Zane, I would just do and say whatever I thought Karl would. That was what made me make the offer to stop, which was obviously the right thing to do. *Hmm. Maybe this whole mate thing wouldn't be that hard after all. Just channel my inner Karl.*

With a loud groan, Zane stood up about ten minutes later. Putting his hands on his hips, he arched backwards and popped his back. I reached up to do a drool check, as I watched his lithe body flex backward like that. Hearing a chuckle, I glanced over to see Karl shaking his head at me.

"You guys ready? I can do this now, you said it's only a quarter mile or so, right?"

"That is correct, sweetest." Karl gracefully stood and stretched, giving me another sexy show. Fuck. I was never going to make it until tonight, if I didn't get my hormones under control and quit acting like a horny teenager. "It should take us about a half hour though, given the steep climb on this final part of our journey."

Turning to me, Karl extended a hand. I took it, and when

he pulled me up, he jerked me against him for a quick kiss before we started loading ourselves up like pack mules again.

Zane had his backpack on, and was already trudging ahead in the direction that we'd been headed when we stopped. The air was much cooler up here, but we were all dripping with sweat when we finally got to our campsite.

The sound of the rushing water falling over the rocks into the river was music to my ears. I looked around, at once feeling calm and settled. Every time I came here, it was like this for me. It was almost as if I'd come home again.

We were only a five minute walk from the falls. Some might find the sound irritating, but I'd always been lulled by its white noise running in the background.

Our campsite was about thirty feet away from the river. Karl liked to dig our fire-pit in the dirt at the edge of the riverbank, while our tent and the rest of the campsite would be set up on the grassy area that bordered it.

There were trees all around us here, we were in the mountains after all. The area where we set up our camp was open, so that we could look up and see the stars overhead, rather than just a canopy of trees. This was Karl's and my special spot, and I hoped that Zane would come to love it as much as we did.

I glanced over to see Zane sniffing the fresh air, and

looking all around with wide eyes. "What's wrong, Gingersnap? Not used to air this clear?"

"Right? I can't believe how gorgeous it is up here! I thought our woods around the lodge were beautiful, but this just takes the cake."

My heart about stopped when he walked across the clearing and stood near the edge of the mountain. He hopped up on a large rock, and looked down over the trail that we'd just climbed.

Before I gathered my wits to react, Karl was already over there, wrapping his arms around Zane's waist to safely anchor him. It was amusing how it took Zane standing on a fucking boulder to actually match Karl in height. Their foot and a half height difference was never so apparent as at that moment.

I grabbed my phone out of my pocket and snapped a picture of them. They were beautiful, standing there overlooking miles of mountain scenery with the bright blue sky overhead. Zane's back to Karl's chest, his small red head resting against Karl's massive shoulder. I looked back down at my phone with a grin and immediately made that image my background pic.

Snagging my water bottle, I walked over and stood next to them. I put my arm around Karl and leaned my head against his shoulder, my face inches away from Zane's. In this quiet moment, I could see an inkling of what we might be able to have together.

With a regretful sigh, I leaned over and kissed Zane's cheek before pulling away. "Hey, guys? I hate to be the party pooper, but we really need to get our campsite set up."

Karl turned, gently scooping Gingersnap up over his arm. "You are right, Owen. This is important."

Setting Zane down, Karl leaned down and spoke softly in his ear. "I do not wish to offend you, sweetest. But I wish to make a request."

Zane turned and looked up at Karl.

"I do not wish to suggest that you might not be strong or graceful, but it would make my bear happy if you did not ever go over by the edge like that again. Not by yourself, that is. I would not like to see you injured, sweetest."

Zane blushed. Rather than his usual snarky response, he admitted with an embarrassed grin, "Crap. I'm sorry. I didn't even think about that! I am so clumsy too, I'm like the *last* person who should be standing on a friggin' rock at the edge of a cliff. Dang, how did I not fall off the mountain? That's like, a record for me or something."

With a smirk, I said, "You didn't go over because Karl was right there to hold you in place. But yeah, maybe not make us turn gray before we're thirty? I'm pretty sure my heart stopped for a second there when you jumped up on that fucking rock."

Zane rolled his eyes at me, but gave Karl a quick hug. "Thank you, Karl."

Karl smiled softly at him, his eyes glowing with the same affection for Zane that I was already feeling so strongly myself. *How had I ever thought that I could live without an omega?* I hadn't even fucked him yet, and he already had me wrapped around his delicate little pinkie finger.

Shaking my head, I pulled out the tent and began the tedious process of setting it up. It was a large one, and would be more than comfortable for the three of us to sleep in tonight. Thinking about sleeping with both of my mates tonight had me picking up the pace, quickly snapping the poles into place and pounding in the stakes.

By the time I was done, Karl had the camp stove set up and was digging a fire pit, while Zane was busily collecting firewood. The large cooler that Karl had carted up the mountain was lined up next to the stove, with the bag of kitchen utensils and dishes resting neatly on the open bottom shelf of the stove.

Zane dropped an armful of wood next to where Karl knelt setting up the fire. Looking around, he asked, "Do we have food for dinner, or are we fishing for our supper?"

"I brought a bunch of hot dogs," I replied. "But fresh fish would be awesome. We don't have any poles though."

Zane shrugged, and pulled his shirt over his head, dropping it down on the ground at his feet. My mouth went dry as I took in his tightly toned body. I had known that he was a little guy, and hadn't expected to see the firm muscles that had been hidden under his shirt.

I gulped, biting down on my fist when his thumbs snagged the waist of his jeans and began pushing them down his freckled thighs, revealing his cute, pink dick and tight balls.

Zane looked over as he kicked his pants to the side, along with his shoes. He looked irritated. "Problem with something over there, Owen?"

Before I could remember how to talk, Karl answered smoothly from where he knelt beside Zane.

"I believe that Owen is affected by your sudden nudity, sweetness. He is not complaining, trust me."

Zane looked confused, as he glanced over at me, and then back at Karl. "Seriously? But I'm just gonna shift so I can fish, I wasn't trying to be weird or anything."

Fucking Karl reached over and ran a large hand up the back of Zane's leg, stopping to rest his hand on the curve of what I could only imagine right now was a perfectly rounded, milky-white ass. I glared at him, pissed that he got to be the first to touch our omega.

Karl looked back at me with a hint of reprimand in his eyes at the jealousy I was putting out there. He looked up at Zane, after first taking a lingering look over his body.

"We are sorry, sweetness. It is simply that Owen and I are both enthralled by your beautiful little body."

"Seriously?" Zane gaped down at him. "You guys are both totally built and super hot. I'm the odd man out in this group. Besides, who wants to look at my pasty flesh and all these freckles?"

Finding my voice, I stood and sauntered over to him while I spoke. "I do. I want to look at your tight little body all day, I would love to spend hours licking my way across your body, while I play connect the dots with your sexy freckles."

Zane blinked several times, standing there frozen in place. I glanced down at Karl, who was looking up at the both of us. Oh, yeah. He was definitely on board with my idea of playing connect the dots. I bet he was already planning to join me on a joint assault. Hmm. There were a lot of freckles, plenty to share.

My little gingersnap made a mewling noise, his body quivering as he stood there on shaky legs. Karl stretched his long arm up and gripped the back of Zane's neck, instantly calming him.

"Breathe, sweetness. There is no need to be nervous, we are your mates. We will treasure you, as you will discover with time. But for now, why don't you go ahead and start fishing? I will come and join you once I have the fire prepared for later."

Zane nodded. He took a couple steps back, then bent

over and smoothly transitioned into a gorgeous, lean wolf. The coloring in his fur was magnificent. The base coat was a deep chocolate brown. The threads of copper, auburn, and lighter shades of cocoa that ran through it though? Amazing. My wolf was doing his best to push forward, wanting desperately to go run with our mate.

"His wolf is as beautiful as the man inside, yes?"

I looked over to Karl standing next to me. Nodding, I reached out my hand for his, threading our fingers together while we watched Zane prancing about in the shallow water.

"I'm sorry, Karl."

He turned and looked at me, then slowly nodded acceptance. "Ah, you mean for the jealousy? Yes, we cannot have that, if we are to be a united trio."

"I wasn't jealous that you were touching him. I was jealous that I wasn't. If that makes sense? I like the idea of us both being with him, and it's hot when I watch you kiss him. My wolf just didn't care for you touching him first."

"You do realize, that there will be times that you will be with him, and I may not be there? Or the reverse, where I am there, but you are not. These are things that we will need to work out among the three of us. But first, we must not scare the little guy. He was aroused just now, but he was also frightened terribly."

"Yeah, I know. Shit, Karl. How the fuck do I know how to

romance a virgin? Maybe I should just bow out until tomorrow? Maybe go on a hike or something, and let you deflower him before I scare him off sex forever. I mean, all I did was talk about licking his milky skin and he was terrified as hell."

Karl chuckled, "Your eyes were predatory, my love. You were looking at him like he was your dinner."

I waggled my brows and smirked. "Mmm, well, I could make a meal out of that tight little body, can't deny that."

Karl shook his head at me. "Owen, my love. The secret to virgins is to not scare them, but to ease them into the idea while showering them with affection."

"I'm not good at affection. I can fuck like a champ, but I'm not the cuddler that you are, babe."

"You sell yourself short, my love. You are quite affection-ate, you just do not care to risk being the first to show it. I would advise you to put your fears aside, and demon-strate your affections to Zane. It will help us tonight. And do not dare think of slinking off in the dark. We both need to be there when we introduce our omega to the wonders of mating. It will set the stage for our relation-ship, yes?"

I took a deep breath. "But what if I fuck it up? I don't wanna freak him out again. That was awful, seeing him shake like that."

Karl pressed his lips to my temple, giving me a gentle kiss.

"I will be there, my love. Just follow my lead, and let your heart guide you with the rest. We will be fine, of this I have no doubt."

"Because you've decided it will work out, so it will?"

"No, my love. Because fate has brought us together. If we believe that, then it only follows that things will work out for us, yes?"

"Yeah. Now, one of us should really strip down and go join him, before he drowns or something."

"I will help him fish, while you air out the sleeping bags and finish setting up our campsite, yes?"

"Figures. You get the fun, and I get the work."

"Owen, my love? I am only assisting with the fishing, because I wish for us to eat tonight. We both know that you would only end up playing with Zane, and we would all end up eating hot dogs for dinner."

I opened my mouth to make a wiener joke, but Karl flashed me a playfully knowing glare as he ripped his shirt off and tossed it over with Zane's. Making a show of zipping my lips, I stepped back and enjoyed the show of watching Karl strip. It was always amazing to watch that sexy bodybuilder sized man get naked and shift into a bear.

Anyone who didn't know Karl would be intimidated by his bear, but it was as gentle as the man inside. I smiled as his body smoothly morphed into the huge bear, reaching a hand out to scratch behind his cute little round ears. He rubbed his side up against my arm while passing me to join Zane.

I gave a hard smack to his big, furry butt as it went by. He turned and flashed his long, sharp teeth at me, but the humor in his eyes ruined any attempt at scaring me.

After the housework of setting up the campsite was done, I sat down on one of the logs that I'd placed in a semi-circle around the fire-pit. From here, I could watch the small wolf playing in the water with the large bear. It was cute.

Fuck. How did I go in the course of a single day, from not ever wanting an omega, to actually planning to mate with one? And now I was noticing that he was cute? The guys back at the lodge would give me so much shit if they could see me now. The craziest part, I realized as I mulled it over, is that I didn't care.

I'm actually happy right now. In this moment, I felt complete in a way that I hadn't even known was possible. And we hadn't even sealed the deal yet. How fucking whole would I feel when I was locked permanently into a sacred bond with these two men? I couldn't wrap my brain around it.

CHAPTER 6

KARL

"You want another marshmallow, Gingersnap?"

I watched as Owen fussed over our omega, touched by how gentle he was being without even realizing it. My love was like that though, thoughtful without being aware of his own consideration. He had an image of himself as being an ignorant, unlovable jock. I knew better, of course. And I had faith that Zane would soon see this in our Owen as well.

"Dude. If I have another one, I'll explode."

"Right, because you've eaten *so* much food tonight."

"Owen, do you not realize that I don't need as much food as you do? I'm literally half your size, man."

"My size? You're half the size of Jake's latest pup!"

"Oh, shut up. Besides, you don't seem to mind my size

that much. Don't think that I haven't seen you checking me out all night."

"What? I'm just sitting here, being nice, offering to roast you another marshmallow. And now you're gonna accuse me of perving on you?"

"I didn't say you were perving. I said you were checking me out. Those are two separate things."

I listened to the entertaining discussion, content to let them find a way to get along. It was good that Zane was relaxing enough to tease Owen now. My heart warmed, watching my mates interact. I knew that they were both at ease with me, it was each other that they needed to be comfortable with now.

After they sat there bantering a little longer, I stood up and stretched. It was time to move things along, and I could smell Zane's interest increasing now. Owen was always just this side of aroused, as was I.

"Would either of you care to go for a walk in the woods, or lay back and count stars? Or shall we retire for the evening?"

Zane looked confused, so Owen cleared it up.

"What the big guy is asking is if you want to take a romantic walk or do some cuddling under the stars. Or, do you want to just get naked and explore each other instead?"

I bit back a smile at Owen's words.

"Umm... I mean, is it up to me?"

"Yeah, Gingersnap. Karl is the romantic one, not me, that's why he gave you the choices. He knows better than to ask me. Who wants woods or stars if there's sex on the menu, am I right?"

Zane blushed. "I w-w-wouldn't know."

"About the romantic shit or the sexy stuff?"

"Either?"

Owen gaped, and I just walked over and scooped Zane up in my arms. He was so light, I could carry him around all day and not break a sweat.

"What's h-h-happening?"

"Come along, Owen. We are going for a walk. If our omega has not yet experienced romance, we are not proceeding to the next step just yet."

"See, Gingersnap? Big guy is the romantic one," Owen said as he kicked some sand over our fire while I waited. Once the fire was banked, he walked over and put his arm around my waist. "Falls?"

"That sounds like a good place to start," I agreed.

"Umm, how far away are we going? Because you really don't have to carry me. I can walk," Zane said nervously to me as we began walking through our shortcut to the falls.

"Yes, you could. But you do not know the area like Owen and I do. I would not care to see you be injured if you tripped over a tree root or large rock in the dark."

"Karl, you do know that we wolves have excellent night vision, right? Even in our human form?"

I thought to myself that if excellent vision did not preclude my little wolf from tripping over his own feet in broad daylight, there was no way that he would safely make it up a steep climb to the waterfalls in the dark.

Those were not thoughts that I felt prudent sharing, so I wisely kept my mouth shut. Instead, I gave him an enigmatic smile and kept walking. Owen knew me well enough to know exactly what I was thinking, and I could hear his muffled laughter as he walked ahead of us up the trail.

Zane gave up his small protest, and wrapped his thin arms around my neck. His cheek rested on my shoulder as he nestled against me, teasing my alpha gland with each exhaled breath. The fact that he was unaware of how he was affecting me only made it that much more exciting.

The sound of the waterfalls was much louder as we stepped out of the trees and got close enough that the fine spray of water misting the air was dampening our skin.

"My turn, let me carry him on my back while we climb up."

"Do I get a say? What if I want to climb up myself?"

"Sorry, Gingersnap. These rocks are slippery, and dangerous enough in the daylight. I wouldn't feel right risking you falling. Now, allow me to rephrase that. Zane, would you like a piggyback ride up to the top of the falls?"

"Okay. I can't turn down such a gallant request without looking like a brat, now can I?"

Owen grinned and turned his back to us so that Zane could climb on. Once he was firmly in place, with his arms and legs wrapped around Owen's neck and waist, we moved on.

The steep climb was treacherous, especially if you didn't know the terrain. Owen had not been exaggerating about that part. We quickly made our way up, being quite familiar with the route. Once we made it to the ledge that was just under the top of the ridge, we walked along the stone path that would take us to a deeper part of the ledge that sat behind the curtain of flowing water.

The stone path and ledge had been cut out over time from the water itself. From this vantage point, it was as if you were standing on the top of the world, looking down over all of creation. I never felt so small, and yet so victorious, as when I stood on this isolated spot overlooking the mountain and river below.

We stepped behind the curtain of flowing water, into the stone chamber. Not quite a cave, it was more an opening in the cliff that was at least a foot higher than the top of my head, and went back a good fifteen feet into the cliff. There were boulders and stones of varying sizes scattered around. Owen and I often used them as chairs after our hikes up here.

Tonight, Owen backed up to one of the the boulders that was about a foot off the ground. I helped Zane slip down from his back, and made sure that he was steady on the stone perch before Owen stepped away. Standing behind Zane, I was amused to notice that even with the added height, he was still a bit shorter than me.

I wrapped my arms around his slender waist, resting my chin on his shoulder as we looked out through the four foot separation between the falls right in front of us. Zane gasped with wonder as he looked out over the moonlit view. The stars sparkled overhead, and the full moon made the landscape easy to see, especially with our enhanced shifter vision.

"What is this place? It's magical!"

"Isn't it cool? Karl showed me this spot when he found me camping up here a couple years ago."

"These are known to my people as the Bearclaw Falls, because the four falls flowing over the rocks in perfect symmetry remind us of the stripes that our claws leave behind."

"Umm, it sounds like this is your special place though. Isn't it kinda weird to bring me here?"

I nuzzled his neck, hating the uncertainty in his voice. I was thinking of how to best answer him, when Owen surprised me by doing it instead.

"Zane, I think the point of Karl wanting us to bring you here was to include you. We don't want to have any special spots that don't belong to all three of us equally from now on. This spot feels sacred to us, and by bringing you here, we are showing you that you are part of us now."

Pressing a kiss to his omega gland, I spoke softly into Zane's ear.

"Owen is correct, sweetness. I would never want you to feel excluded in our relationship. From now on, we are three united, yes? I cannot deny that Owen and I have shared a special relationship, but now we will share that with you. As an equal partner. It is not my wish that any of us should feel themselves less than the others. I believe that this is the only way that this will work, yes?"

Owen stepped up in front of Zane, wrapping his arms around both of us with his arms loosely sandwiching Zane between our bodies.

"I agree with what Karl said. I love him, Zane. But I also want to love you as well. I feel the connection getting stronger every minute, do you feel it too?"

Zane nodded, his face barely an inch from Owen's now. He leaned forward and tentatively kissed Owen's lips. I bit back a moan as I watched Owen deepen that kiss, tilting his face to drive his tongue into Zane's mouth. I knew how hard and fast my love's kisses were. Already, I could feel its effect on Zane.

Arousal spiked through his gingersnap scent, making it spicier and more fragrant. Scraping my teeth gently over his omega gland, I felt him shiver under my touch. I unfastened his pants, shoving them down over his hips to bare his slim cock.

I wrapped my hand around his length, slowly stroking it while I watched my mates kiss. Zane rocked into my hand. I stroked slowly to let him learn my touch. I still had one hand free to jerk open my pants. My hard dick burst free of its denim jail. I pushed myself between his round butt cheeks, rutting into his crack. My dick moved in perfect sync with his dick in my hand.

I moved my free hand back to rest on Zane's hip as Owen's hands came down to cup my ass. This pulled me closer against Zane, pushing my cock deeper between his cheeks.

Owen broke their kiss long enough to say, "Pull my dick out, babe! Jack me together with Gingersnap."

He went back to kissing Zane, while I used my free hand to open Owen's jeans and pull his cock out. I somehow managed to not miss a stroke when he thrust his cock into my loose fist to rub against Zane's. Stroking them together, I watched their cocks rub against each other in my fist.

Their cock-heads shoved up against each other, as they fought to push up through the opening in my fist. Their honey was seeping through their slits and coating my hand. Zane broke their kiss, his head falling back against my shoulder. Owen leaned around him, firmly pressing his lips to mine.

Our tongues battled for dominance as teeth scraped in our passionate lip-lock. Zane grunted, his head twisting from side to side. Seconds later, a gush of white nectar flooded over my fist, coating their cocks as Zane came hard. Owen gave a few frantic thrusts, and spurted gobs of hot cum.

While he was cumming, I sped up my own thrusts. Right as Owen's seed was spilling over my fist, I shot mine onto Zane's back. We broke our kiss, Owen pulling back first. He tucked his cock away, then carefully pulled up Zane's pants. I watched my nectar sliding down his crack as his pants came up.

It satisfied me to know that Zane would be leaving with my seed coating his ass. I stood there with my cock hanging out, and brought my hand up to lick my lovers' combined juices that still coated my skin.

Zane watched me with wide eyes. Owen chuckled at his expression, and leaned over to take his own taste from my hand. Not wanting to exclude him, Owen swiped his thumb across my hand and held it to Zane's lips. After a brief hesitation, his pink tongue flicked out to lap the cream from Owen's thumb.

Owen watched him through hooded eyes. "Fuuuck. If I hadn't just shot my load, I think I'd come on the spot from watching you do that, Gingersnap."

Zane looked back and forth between Owen and me before glancing down at the cum splattered shirt he still wore. Chuckling, his only response was to say, "I think I need to go change my shirt now."

* * *

We finally made it back to our campsite an hour or so later. We had lost track of time, sitting together behind the falls. We had kissed and made out with each other, but nothing more. Owen and I were on the same page about easing our nervous omega into the carnal part of our relationship.

Owen set Zane down; this time he had carried him all the way from the falls to our camp. We proceeded to strip down before crawling into the tent. Zane watched us for a moment, as if unsure what to do, then he calmly began to strip as well.

I went in first, and settled myself down on my side at the far left of the tent flap. Owen followed me in, sliding to the right. We both propped ourselves up on our elbows, and waited for Zane. We looked over at each other, sharing a smile at what we both knew was to come.

"Owen," I said quietly. "I want you to give him your knot."

"What? But what about you?"

"I will find my own pleasure from watching you. But since neither of us has ever experienced a knot, since we've never mated, we have no idea how large they will be. I'm assuming, if it goes along with our general size, that mine will be larger, yes?"

Owen nodded in understanding. "Yeah, let's not break our omega the first night we get him, huh?"

We grinned at each other, knowing that omegas were built to take their alphas' knots, yet neither of us wanting to hurt him during his first mating. I sat up, wondering what was keeping Zane, when the tent was suddenly filled with the enticing scent of omega heat pheromones.

Owen looked over at me, suddenly sitting up in alarm.

"Is that what I think it is?"

"Yes, our omega has gone into heat. One of us needs to get him, he may be confused or frightened."

"Damn, that's intense," he said as he began to open the flap and crawl out in search of Zane. "No wonder the other alphas lose their shit around an omega in heat. Good thing I'm already attached to him, Karl."

"Why is that, Owen?" I asked with concern, as he began to crawl out of the tent.

Looking back over his shoulder, he said, "Because otherwise, I don't think I could be gentle like I want to be. But you'll make sure I keep my cool, right?"

"Count on it, my love."

He nodded, and disappeared into the night in search of our omega mate.

CHAPTER 7

OWEN

When I emerged from our tent, I immediately spotted Zane lying on the ground. He was in the same spot where he'd been undressing when I'd gone inside. I realized that he was writhing there, as if in pain.

I froze, not sure what was happening. His whimpering moan caught my attention. Crawling to him, I crossed the four feet that separated us. I brushed the back of my hand against his flushed forehead, concerned by how feverish he seemed.

As soon as I touched him, his body reacted. He began humping the air, while his hands reached out mindlessly for a body to grab.

He gasped out in need, "I need you, alpha. Want your knot. Please. Fuck my hole, alpha."

I paused, unsure how to proceed, because this was definitely not normal behavior for my introverted little Gingersnap.

"Pick him up, and get him inside, Owen. His heat has overpowered his mind right now. It is our job to take care of his needs, yes?"

Hearing Karl, I put a hand under Zane's back and the other under his upper thighs, and lifted him. Cradling him against my chest, I knee-walked back to the tent opening. Karl held the flap open while I carried him inside.

Zane turned and wrapped his arms around my neck, burying his face over my alpha gland. He squirmed until his lower half slipped free of my arm, and knelt in front of me. Grinding against me, his hands clawed the back of my shoulders while he sucked hard against my alpha gland.

"Karl? A little help?"

"Lay him down. Together we will prepare him for your knot, my love."

My heart raced as I laid our omega down on the sleeping bag. Prying his hands from around my neck, I leaned back against my heels. Karl leaned over Zane's chest and sucked on one of his tiny, pink nipples. His other hand reached over to flick and tease the other nipple. Zane moaned loudly, spreading his legs while humping the air.

I watched as his clear slick seeped from his pink hole. I'd

always been curious about the self-lubricating omega channel, but this was the first time I had seen it in person. Curious, I stretched out a finger and scooped some up.

I brought my finger to my nose first, inhaling the sweet smell first before I licked it clean. Zane's entire body was flushed pink now. He hand wrapped around his dick, jerking himself while Karl teased his nipples.

"Karl, are you sure I should do this right now?"

Karl popped his mouth off the nipple he was suckling. He spoke in a hoarse voice as he answered, "Zane needs you, Owen. He gave his consent already, now help him. This is hurting him, can you not see his need?"

Biting my lip, I pushed his knees up and out to the side. I lined my cock up against his hole, wondering if I should ease in, or go in one thrust. Without warning, Zane pumped his hips up against mine. He impaled himself on my cock.

I gripped his hips, holding him in place. Zane may not have needed a moment at this point, but I did. The heat inside his body was overwhelming against my shaft. I caught my breath, then slowly began to fuck him.

Thrusting slowly at first, my cock slid easily in and out of his slippery hole. I released his hips, sliding my hands around to cup his ass cheeks. Lifting his ass up, I changed my angle to please him. He screamed out when my tip slid over that spongy nerve bundle. I smirked, well aware of how good it felt to have that magical prostate massaged.

Moving faster, I rocked in and out. Each pass rubbed against his magic spot. His moans grew louder with each pump of my hips. Rocking faster now, I fucked him fast and hard. His hips jerked back against me, seeking more. I grunted as I thrust in deeper.

I didn't notice the base of my cock as it began to swell. When I was unable to pull out finally, I glanced down. Realizing that I had actually popped a knot for the first time was too much. I exploded into Zane's body, with a gushing flood of alpha seed.

"Karl! I need to bite him!"

Karl quickly moved, clearing my path to Zane's omega gland. I got hit in the face by a splat of cum, when his cock erupted right as I was leaning over. In my need to claim him, I was barely aware of him coming.

Focused on giving him my bite, I almost missed his returning bite. A swirling confusion of things happened all at once. My elongated fangs pierced his flesh, and I tasted his blood on my tongue. A sharp pain quickly turned to pleasure, as his fangs broke through the skin of my own alpha gland.

I felt our spirits click together all at once. I could feel his pleasure from my knot rubbing against his prostate as I humped him. It was surreal, but I felt as if I were fucking and being fucked all at once. I didn't realize that being bonded meant that we would feel the pleasure and pain each other felt.

As I came back to my own senses, it dawned on me that our bond was incomplete. Something was missing. Had I done it wrong? Then I realized, no. *Someone* was missing. I needed to claim Karl now.

I rolled over on my back, carefully bringing the now sleeping Zane along with me to rest on my chest. Fenris only knew how long that we would be locked together. Settling him so that my knot wasn't pulling on his hole, I looked over at Karl. He was jerking himself in a steady rhythm, clearly turned on from watching our mating.

"Karl. I need you to join our bond, it is incomplete. Feed your dick into my mouth, babe. When you come, pull out and bite me. And let me bite you."

"And what of Zane?"

"You can share the claiming bite when he takes your knot next."

His hand moved faster on his leaking shaft. "I like the idea that each of our shoulders will carry dual bite marks, yes?"

I grinned, stretching a hand toward his hip as he knee-walked over to feed me his cock. Opening wide, I took him into my mouth, sucking hard. I could tell it wouldn't take much, he was already right there on the cusp. My hand came up to fondle his balls, lightly squeezing him between my fingers.

Hollowing my cheeks, I sucked hard as he thrust into my mouth. After four quick pumps, he growled loudly. Cum shot into my mouth and ran down my throat. Jerking himself free, he bent over and sank his teeth into my alpha gland. I felt myself shooting another load of my seed into Zane, while I pushed Karl's head to the side and bit down on his alpha gland.

Again, the surreal swirl of sensations overwhelmed me as the missing piece of my bond clicked into place. I licked the blood away from where I'd bitten him. Turning to look into his eyes, I could feel his pure love washing over me. Lifting my chin, I sought his lips.

His lips crashed down over mine, a bit rougher than was his norm. I felt completely whole as I kissed him. Finally, I had my forever home with these two men. Breaking our kiss, I touched my forehead to his. I didn't realize that I had been crying until he turned to lick the trail of my tears away.

"That. That was just beautiful, Karl. I can feel you, inside my soul. You are there now."

Smiling softly, he said, "Yes, my love. And I also feel you inside of me. This is wonderful, yes?"

"Yes," I agreed. "We should have done this a long time ago."

"That would not have been possible, my love." He turned to press a kiss on the top of Zane's head. Then he stretched out to lay beside us, with his head on my chest next to Zane. "We were missing a piece of us until today."

"Yeah, we really were. I can't wait for you and Zane to bond, his spirit is so fucking pure, babe. He is every bit as beautiful as you said. I never thought I would feel this way for an omega, but I can't imagine how I ever lived without him before now."

"That is because he was meant to be ours, yes? This is why he is our fated-mate, my love. We are all made perfect together, and only for each other. No other omega would have made you feel this way, because they were not meant for you."

Zane started to stir, blinking his eyes open. When he saw Karl, a smile lit up his face.

"I can feel you, Karl. Through my bond to Owen, I feel you."

He moved his hand up to rest on Karl's cheek. Karl leaned into that small palm, practically purring as he rubbed against it.

"I cannot wait to feel you completely, sweetness. This is but a shadow of what our own bond will be, yes?"

Zane nodded thoughtfully. "Yeah, my bond to Owen is way stronger. It will be good when we share the same."

I felt my dick hardening as Zane squirmed to kiss Karl.

With a grunt, I said, "If you want my knot to ever go down enough for you guys to get your turn, then you should probably quit moving. And maybe not kiss each other so much."

Karl grinned and Zane giggled, both of them feeling my arousal through our bonds. The sight of Gingersnap's lips meeting Karl's as the bear moved closer didn't help slow my erection. Nope. Watching my mates laying across my chest and making out only made me harder. Yeah. This was gonna be a long fucking night. Pun totally intended.

The next morning, I woke up to find myself intertwined with Owen. I smiled when I smelled bacon cooking outside the tent. I reached out across my new bond to Karl, sending love to him.

Moments later, his head popped through the flap. Meeting my eyes, he smiled happily.

"I will let you be the one to risk waking our mate. He is more of a bear in the morning than I am, but he is unlikely to hurt you. I think he likes you too much, yes?"

I rolled my eyes. "No. I think he's just afraid that I'm gonna break or something because I'm so much smaller than you guys."

"If last night's workout didn't break you, or at least split your ass open, then I'm pretty sure that you're stronger than you look," Owen grumbled out as he turned to kiss me good morning.

Turning back to Karl, he playfully glared as he spoke, "And what the fuck, babe? You trying to make me look like an asshole to Zane already?"

Elbowing him in the side, I said, "As if I need Karl to tell me that. Ever spend five minutes with yourself?"

Owen flipped me over, leaning over me with his weight braced on his hands. "Watch out, Gingersnap."

"Or what?"

"Or you might get another lesson in how much you love me. Or maybe you just love my cock. Either way, I know you want me."

I giggled, running my hands over his broad chest. Karl cleared his throat pointedly, smirking at us both as he tossed the clothes at our heads that we'd left outside the tent last night.

"I am about to serve breakfast. I do not wish for it to burn or grow cold because my mates are knotted together and unable to join me. I suggest that you table this for now, pull on some pants, and come outside."

"He's just jealous that I'm cuddled up with you and he's stuck cooking," Owen said in a loud stage whisper.

Rolling my eyes, I whisper-yelled back, "Maybe so, but at

least one of us got our ass out of bed and saw to the food situation."

I heard Karl laughing outside, his shifter ears easily hearing us talk. Owen grinned and rolled off to put on his jeans. I wasn't aware I was staring until my own jeans landed against my chest.

"Quit undressing me with your eyes! I'm already fighting hard enough to be good!" Owen grinned, and pointed at my jeans.

"Please just get those on and quit tempting me, Ginger-snap. Karl's waiting, and we don't want our food to be ruined. Trust me, that bear can cook."

I pulled my pants on slowly, under Owen's watchful gaze. It felt good to know that the big alpha found my body so sexy. It dawned on me as I crawled out of the tent behind him that I felt completely normal.

"Karl, should I be feeling so good right now? I mean, how long does heat usually last? Or do you even know?"

Karl cocked his head at me, and inhaled deeply, smelling the air. Opening his eyes, he merely pointed at the log behind him.

"Come, sweetest. Sit down and allow me to feed you. You must be quite famished now, yes?"

Through our bond, I could tell that Karl was holding something back and Owen was starting to panic. Looking back and forth between them, it dawned on me what was going on. I dropped my ass down on the log with a loud thump, and simply said, "Fuck me."

Both alphas turned their heads toward me, looking me over and reaching across our bond to assess me. Karl immediately knew that I had correctly guessed what was going on and replied, "I believe that we already did that last night, yes?"

Owen snorted. "Oh, shit. Karl just made a joke! Make a note of this, Gingersnap, because he doesn't do that often."

Karl flipped Owen off playfully, and turned to get my food. Owen laughed harder as he came over to sit down beside me. Putting his arm around my shoulder, he pulled me against him. I rested my head on his shoulder, my mind racing with the implications of all this.

"It's okay, Zane. We'll figure it out together, that's why there's three of us, right? It's not that I don't like pups, didn't I tell you that? Besides, the idea of a little ginger-snap running around is strangely appealing now."

Karl sat down beside me, the plate in his hand piled high with food. The look on my face made him chuckle, and he said, "I made one plate for us all to share while we talk. I promise that this is not all intended for only you."

Relieved, I picked up a toasted egg sandwich and nibbled at it. Owen and Karl dug into the bacon. Owen got up and went over to fill cups of coffee for each of us. After he was seated again, I spoke up finally.

"Karl? You can smell any hormonal changes, like Doc does?"

"Yes, sweetness. It is a bear thing, as Owen would say."

"Uh-huh. And I'm already pregnant? That's for sure what you smelled? It's why my heat is over almost before it began?"

"Yes. We bears can tell hours after conception, Zane. I can definitely smell that you are now carrying our child."

I nodded, unsure how I felt about that. As much as I loved pups, could I handle the loss of another family member should something happen to it? But then, hadn't I already opened the door to possible loss by accepting the claim of my mates? I hugged myself, pulling my knees up to my chest.

Karl passed the food to Owen. Silently, he turned and scooped me up into his lap. I cuddled into him, while still curled into a defensive ball.

"Talk to me, sweetest. Tell me what is troubling you. Did you not wish for us to have a young one yet? Perhaps we should have discussed it more, yes?"

"That's not it," I mumbled against his chest. "I love pups, or cubs, I guess. Whatever we get, I will love it."

"Then what is the problem? Are you concerned about Owen? He is not unhappy, he just needs to adjust to the idea."

Shaking my head, I felt the tears streaming down my face as I said, "What if I lose you guys? Or our child? There's a reason that I don't open my heart, Karl. I can't risk it, and I know better! I haven't been close to anybody in over three years. And now, I let myself just go off and get bonded and knocked up! There's no turning back from this, and if I lose any of you, I will die this time."

Karl stroked my back with one hand, while holding me close with the other. He didn't interrupt, but instead let me collect myself enough to finish my thoughts as I sobbed in his lap. After I calmed, I finished my thoughts.

"I had a family once, and they were all stolen from me at the same time. I said good-bye that morning, and left with my friends to go to graduation practice. I don't remember if I even told my mom that I loved her. My dad was still in bed, and my brother was giving me shit about whether I was tall enough to reach the steps to the podium when I collected my diploma."

I smiled sadly, remembering my brother's constant teasing. "I didn't know that they weren't there, until nobody cheered when my name was called. I knew right then that something bad had happened. I took my diploma, and left. I didn't even finish the ceremony."

Owen came over and crouched beside us. I turned my face to look at him, surprised by the empathy that I saw in his eyes. He bit his lip and put his hand on my thigh. Looking down, he cleared his throat before he spoke.

"Zane. I'm so sorry that you had to go through that, baby. I hate that you are the sole survivor of such a happy family. Your brother was fucking awesome. He was always joking around, and making all of us laugh. Will it piss you off if I make a suggestion?"

"Maybe." I shrugged. "Depends on what you have to say."

"I'm not gonna belittle your loss by comparing it to my life, or even Karl's, because there's no comparison. You had the perfect family. I had no family. Karl has a family that doesn't bother to talk to him, a twin brother that doesn't answer a simple text. We all share pain and loneliness when it comes to family. My suggestion is that you let go of the day that they died, and focus on the time that you did have with them."

I nodded, embarrassed to realize that of the three of us, I was the only one who knew what a loving family felt like.

"No, don't be embarrassed." He grinned at my shocked look. "Bonded now, remember? I can totally feel your emotions, Gingersnap."

Karl chuckled. I sat up, still resting my face against that big chest, but no longer curled up in a ball, as I let my limbs relax.

"Anyway. My point is, remember the happy times with your family. Laugh at the memories of your brother's stupid pranks. Smile when you think of your dad making lame jokes, or your mom's cooking."

"Mom was a lousy cook. She actually burned a pot once while boiling water. We laughed so hard at that."

"See? And doesn't it feel good to smile at that memory?"

I nodded, smiling like he'd pointed out.

Karl said, "I do not understand this thing. How did your mother burn a pot while boiling water?"

Laughing, I explained that she had gotten distracted with a crossword puzzle and the water had all boiled away. The pot had gotten so hot, that it was burned beyond salvation when my dad found it an hour later. We all shared a laugh at my story, and I felt my heart truly opening for the first time since I'd lost my family.

"Karl? Can I ask about your family? I know that Owen is an orphan, but I don't know anything about you."

Karl sighed, then tried to explain.

"We bears are more solitary creatures than you wolves. Once we are grown, our parents encourage us to leave the nest. When my brother and I left home, they sold our family house and bought an RV. They travel around now, if they are even still alive. I haven't seen them in ten years."

"Ten years? Seriously?"

"Yes. We were eighteen when they left, and they have never been in touch. Bear mates have eyes only for each other. The cubs are a responsibility they have to ensure that our lines do not disappear."

"Karl!" I gasped in horror. "That's awful!"

He shrugged. "It is the way of our people. My brother met his mate, and he left me too. That was four years ago now, and I do not know how he fares. I miss my brother. Like Owen said, he is my twin. I have decided that I am a broken bear, because I feel the need for family more than I should."

"No wonder you ended up mated to a couple of wolves then. Fenris gave you to pack animals that have a strong need for family connections."

"So you are not upset about the baby now, yes?"

I rested a protective hand against my flat stomach. "I was never upset about the baby, not really. I am just afraid to lose it, or either of you."

Owen leaned over me to peck Karl on the lips, and then turned back to kiss me. After an uncharacteristically soft kiss, he pulled back and rubbed the tip of his nose against mine briefly.

Pulling himself up to sit beside Karl, Owen said, "Don't be afraid of losing us, because if something happens to one of us, you'll be right there too. I don't think I'll ever be able to let you out of my sight, Gingersnap. You've grown on me like mold this past couple days."

I crinkled my nose, and Karl shook his head chuckling.

"Seriously, Owen, you are so romantic! I'm a mold? Really?"

He grinned, and winked at me proudly. "Yep. You really *grew* on me."

Karl and I both groaned.

* * *

The trip down the mountain was just as long as the trip up. Except this time, I wasn't worried about burning lungs and aching calves. No, this time my fear was tripping and rolling all the way down the mountain like a tumbleweed.

After we made it to the car, I got in my seat and sucked down a bottle of water while the guys loaded up the back with our bags and gear. It had been a beautiful week, and we were all completely bonded in our relationship. We had decided to ask Alpha to let us live in the two bedroom cabin near Doc's place.

I didn't want to be far from our pack, but I just wanted to be with our own growing family. Living next door to Doc would have me close enough if the baby came suddenly, but still give us our own space. Owen needed to be near his friends, but he agreed that this was a good idea.

My grief had kept me from forming close friendships within the pack, and I felt like the odd man out most of the time. I wanted to give them a chance, and work on building community. However, I felt that given our unique situation, we should have our privacy. Maybe later we could rethink things and move into the lodge, but for now, I just needed to be alone with my alphas.

"Hey, Gingersnap. You comfortable back there? What are you so deep in thought about?" My mates had just slid into their seats up front, and were buckling up for the trip home.

"I'm good. I was thinking about the cabin idea, and how much I like it. Am I weird that I don't want to live in the middle of the pack?"

Karl caught my eyes in the rear-view mirror. "I do not think so, not at all. I think that maybe I am a little bit of a wolf at heart, craving pack. Perhaps, you are a little bit of a bear at heart, needing solitude with your mates, yes?"

Smiling, I nodded. "As usual, I think that you're right, Karl. Are you both sure that you'll be okay with not living in the lodge itself?"

Owen looked at me over his shoulder. "Baby, we have a unique set-up in our pack. Most packs are like our old one, where families stayed in their own homes but were close with the community."

"That's true. I feel better now that you mention that. I wonder why our pack is different?"

"Honestly?" Owen looked sad for minute. "You weren't there when we all rescued the omegas from Alpha

Fremont. I mean, I'm glad that you never made it onto his radar. That probably saved you from being another member of his captive harem of breeding stock."

He chewed his lip, looking pensive for a moment. "When we settled here, the omegas needed to be close to each other, and we needed to know that we were protecting them. It was a rough time of transition for them."

Glancing at Karl, he asked, "Did I ever tell you that Jake's daughter, Erin, is actually his niece? She was his twin's baby. He and Kai adopted her after Jenny was killed the day that Alpha Fremont came here with his thugs to try and steal the omegas back."

"Dang, I don't think I even knew about how Jenny died. I knew that Erin was his niece, because Micah and I brought her here with Aries' pups. That's the day that I met Karl."

Karl shook his head, quietly driving while we talked. "I wasn't aware that so much was involved, I only knew that your Alpha needed extra protectors along your borders because you were under threat of attack. I do not believe that I ever knew the reason why, I just volunteered to help."

He shrugged. "I liked your pack so much that I've stayed around ever since."

Owen waggled his brows suggestively. "Well, some of us liked you too."

I laughed at the blush that filled Karl's cheeks. As a blonde, his light skin blushed just as pink as mine did.

"Plus, there's also the fact that most of the pack pups are related. That's probably the biggest reason that they all stayed in the lodge, so that their pups could grow up together."

Karl looked confused, so I explained. "Remember how Owen mentioned that the old Alpha had held those omegas captive for breeding? He sired Erin, our Alpha's niece. Well, daughter now. But, anyway." I shook my head, trying to stay on track.

"The pups that Micah and I brought here with us were also sired by Alpha Fremont. Micah mated their dad, Aries. Aries and Kai are best friends, so they are raising their pups together."

"Don't forget Sy and Brianne," Owen added. "Sy is the third member of that little omega trio. His oldest daughter, Brianne, was also sired by Fremont. Sy mated with my friend, Seth, earlier this year. Even though Micah, Seth, and Jake all have had more pups with their mates, they all respect the fact that their older pups are actually half-siblings."

Karl shook his head. "I cannot believe that I did not know all of this before. You have held out on me, my love. Your pack is almost as good as watching a soap opera, yes?"

I giggled. "Have you met our Alpha's little aunt? She is a freaky old lady."

My eyes widened, and I looked at Owen in horror. "Owen! She's gonna have a field day with our relationship! I can't believe I didn't think about Aunt Kat before, holy crap!"

Owen laughed so hard that he had tears running down his face. At Karl's questioning look, he merely said, "There's no way to properly prepare you for Aunt Kat, so I'm not gonna try. She has to be experienced first hand. I will tell you this though, she's an erotica author and blogger. She reviews adult toys and sex aids on her blog. Oh, and she's in her sixties." He started laughing again at Karl's shocked expression.

I giggled. "Yeah, you should have seen the ginormous bottle of lube that she set down in front of Sy at the freakin' dinner table when he mated Seth. He about died! I would have too, but his face was too funny for words."

Owen's palms smacked his thighs as he gasped for breath. "I had totally forgotten about that! And it had a big red bow tied around it, right? That was fucking hilarious as hell! Shit, remind me to order a bottle of that when we get settled, Gingersnap. It will make an awesome gift for them at Winter Solstice."

I shook my head, but totally filed that idea away. Owen was right, that would be an awesome gift for those two. "Sure thing, babe. And we'll make sure to just tie a bow around it and present it to them at dinner, right?"

"Oh, hell, yeah. We'll make sure to thump it down real

good on the table, hard enough to make the silverware jump!"

Karl shook his head while we laughed our butts off the rest of the way home, telling him funny stories about our pack-mates. I was starting to regret having kept everyone but the pups at arm's length for so long. *Maybe it's time to remedy that*, I thought to myself. Karl craved connection, and that was something that Owen and I could give him. A family that appreciated him and a pack to support him.

We were having such a great time that I didn't notice the serious look on Doc's face when we arrived at home. He came out while the alphas were unloading, with a small girl in his arms. She was obviously a bear cub, I could tell right away.

When I smelled a familiar hint of coconut, I tapped Karl on the shoulder. "Um, babe? I think that Doc Ollie is looking for you. And I'm pretty sure that the cub he's carrying is kin to you."

Karl stood up so fast, he banged his head on the raised lift-gate at the back of the SUV. He looked around the corner of the car, his eyes watering when he saw the cub.

Her cherubic face was framed by the curliest blonde hair that I'd ever seen. She was chattering to Doc in a steady stream of utterly charming ramblings. I couldn't see her eye color from here, but I was willing to bet that it was an exact match to Karl's gray-green beauties.

Karl seemed to be struggling to move, and I could feel the grief flowing through our bond. I slipped my arm around his waist, and guided him around the car. Owen came up on his other side, his hand coming up to wrap around Karl's shoulders. With our support, he walked up to meet Doc.

"Hello, Karl," Doc said kindly, with a friendly nod to Owen and me. "I am sorry to meet you like this. Obviously you know that I have bad news, yes?"

Karl nodded. "How long has the cub been in your care, Ollie?"

"For the past two days. I apologize for not tracking you down, Karl. I just hesitated to ruin your claiming phase. And I was perfectly happy to care for Trixie in your absence."

Karl nodded. "They are both gone then? Kane? His mate?"

"Yes, Karl." Doc took a deep breath, smiling down at the child on his hip. Looking back at us, he said quietly. "There was a fire, about two years ago. Kane brought Trixie out, but he went back in for his mate. She was expecting another cub, so you will understand that he could not walk away without trying to save them both."

"Two years ago, you say? Why has it taken so long for

them to bring her to me? And they did not think to inform me that my brother was gone?"

"She was taken in by her maternal grandmother. She died recently, which is when the Alpha began to search for you. Karl, I do not know why they did not think to inform you when your brother passed. That was not right, my friend."

Karl broke down in tears, saying, "He wasn't ignoring my calls or not texting me. I was so mad at him, but he wasn't ignoring me." I held him for several minutes, then turned him into Owen's arms.

While Owen comforted our mate, I stepped over to talk to Doc and Trixie. I knew that Owen could be there for him, but one of us also needed to greet Trixie. This was definitely a situation where having two mates came in handy.

I smiled at our new cub. She was part of our family now. There would be no question about that.

"Hi, there," I said in a friendly voice. "I'm your Uncle Zane, I'm so happy to meet you, sugarplum."

"Hello, I am Trixie. It is a pleasure to meet you, Uncle." She spoke in the same quaintly proper speech pattern that the other bears I'd met used. I wondered if it was a bear thing, or if it was from the local den's Russian heritage. Either way, I found it oddly charming.

"How old are you, sugarplum?"

"I am three. How old are you?"

Doc bit back a smile, but I answered her honestly. "I'm twenty-one. Is that too young to be an uncle?"

She shook her head solemnly. "No, Uncle. That is more than all of my fingers and toes. This means that you are very old, yes?"

I giggled, and poked a finger out to tickle her chubby little girl belly. "No, I am not very old, you little stinker!"

She giggled then, and a dimple identical to Karl's appeared in her cheek. If I hadn't known that Karl had a twin, I would've been positive that this was his pup. She looked just like a little girl version of my mate.

"Can I hold you, Trixie?"

She looked to Doc for permission, and at his nod, held her little arms out to me. I picked her up, and swung her easily over to my hip. I nuzzled into her sunny curls, loving the silky feel of them against my face.

Doc watched us quietly, as she and I chatted and got comfortable with each other. After a while, she yawned and rested her head against my shoulder. Cuddling her against me, I asked Doc a few pertinent questions.

"Does Trixie understand what is happening?"

"Yes, the den Alpha of her mother's clan explained to her that she would be coming to live with her uncle. When the Alpha of Karl's den called here, I went and picked her up. I thought that was what Karl would want, yes?"

"Yeah, Karl's gonna be settling in here now," I said shyly.

Doc nodded, pointing at my belly. "And I assume that he has already told you that you are carrying, yes?"

"Yeah, don't worry. I'll be coming to see you soon," I promised. My face was pretty red at that point, but that was the curse of being a ginger.

Doc nodded. I asked, "Does Trixie need anything? Did they bring her clothes and toys?"

"She brought along clothing, but she does not have any toys. Apparently, her grandmother was a poor widow woman."

I looked down to see that she had fallen asleep in my arms. I kissed her little cheek. I promised myself that this precious cub would have at least one dolly, and definitely a teddy bear, before bedtime tonight.

"Shall I take her from you, Zane? Her weight will be too taxing for you to hold long, especially in your condition, yes?"

Before I could answer, I felt Trixie being lifted out of my arms. I looked up to see Owen tucking her against his chest. He shrugged at my raised brow.

"We heard Doc. He's right, you don't need to be wearing yourself out."

I felt Karl come up behind me. I stepped back into his arms, leaning into him while he wrapped his arms around me. His chin resting on my head, he held me close, absorbing comfort from me.

"Ollie. I heard your conversation with my mate. I wish to thank you for your help with Trixie. I had forgotten the comfort of having friends in times of need."

Doc nodded. "It was no trouble, Karl. I would like to offer my condolences for your loss. Taking care of your niece was the least that I could do, yes?"

Our Alpha and his second, Daniel, came walking up then. Alpha clapped Doc on the shoulder, before greeting us all with a broad smile.

"Doc here was adamant about watching over Trixie until you came home. I was starting to think that he didn't trust your niece among us wolves, you know?"

He laughed, letting the more literal minded bears know that he was just teasing. Daniel grinned over at Owen, who was standing there cuddling the little frilly ball of sunshine against his chest.

"Owen. First, you get mated to not one, but two mates. And now you're actually cuddling a cub? Damn, I can't believe that you of all people are settling down! What's next? You planning to become a daddy soon?"

My cheeks immediately flushed, giving away our secret as my blushes always tended to do. Daniel gaped for a second, then started roaring with laughter. Jake was cracking up too. I could feel Karl holding back his humor, while I bit my lip. It *was* pretty funny for an alpha like Owen to be settling down so abruptly.

Owen shut them right down, though. He walked over stood next to us, and tilted his chin defiantly. "Yeah, our mate is pregnant. However, it appears that my mates and I already have a cub. Which, if I follow Jake and Kai's example, makes Trixie my daughter now. So tell me, why the fuck wouldn't I cuddle the shit out my own cub?"

I smiled proudly at Owen, loving how he immediately stepped up to claim Karl's niece as our own. I could feel Karl's emotions choking him up. I reached a hand up behind me, and rubbed my fingertips over his alpha gland. It was the only tool in my arsenal that would immediately calm an alpha, but dang, did it ever work.

Alpha Jake hid his laughter in a cough, and said, "Owen? If you're gonna be a daddy? Let me give you a tip. Watch those F-bombs when the cub is awake. Little ones tend to repeat everything they hear. And if my mate hears one of our pups cussing? He will beat the crap out of you, alpha or not."

I giggled, picturing Kai going toe to toe with Owen. Strangely enough, I could almost picture it.

Alpha Jake looked over at Karl now. "Karl, I want to tell you how very sorry I am to hear of your loss. Having lost my own twin, I have the unfortunate privilege of knowing how you feel right now. Just know that my door is always open if you need to talk."

Karl released me, and stepped around to shake hands with Alpha Jake. "Thanks, Alpha. I appreciate your concern. I also wish to thank you for opening your doors to my niece in our absence."

"Seriously? Don't bother thanking me, dude. What kind of dicks wouldn't be there for a child in need? I'm just glad that we were able to be here. Now, I hate to deal with details when I know you want to be alone with your mates and grieve, but we need to get you settled. Have you guys decided where you want to live?"

Owen spoke up and answered. "Jake? If it's okay, I'd like to move our family out to that big cabin down near Doc. We'd be close enough if the cub or Zane need medical care, but far enough to have privacy while we figure our family out. I had already planned to ask you that, but I think with Trixie here it's even more important."

Daniel spoke up with concern. "But you still want to be pack, right?"

"Of course, dumb-ass." Owen rolled his eyes. "Like I told Zane, most packs don't live in one building like ours has been lucky enough to do. But given our unique situation, I want to have a little privacy."

Alpha Jake nodded with complete understanding. "And you'll still run with us on full moons, and work your jobs as patrol guards?"

"Of course, Jake. Nothing is changing, except that Zane and I will be sleeping under a different roof. Oh, and you're adding another bear and a cub to the pack. And either a cub or a pup in three months. Other than that? Business as usual, man."

Alpha Jake shook his head, grinning at my mate. I could see the years of friendship between them as Daniel, Owen, and Alpha Jake all exchanged smiles.

"Well, then, let's get these guys settled down in cabin six," Daniel said, rubbing his hands together. "Let's see, we'll need someone to run over to Wally World and pick up a bed for your cub. Do you guys wanna handle that, or should I send someone?"

At Karl's questioning look, Alpha Jake explained, "Daniel is the one who handles all the detail stuff for the pack. I hate planning, but he thrives on it. He's the organization guy."

Daniel flashed his stiff smile. "Yeah, yeah. Anyway, let's get this figured out. Do one of you guys want to go down there with me, so we can check out the furniture? We can swap anything out from one of the other cabins if you want. I'll get us some manpower together, and we should have you all settled by dinner. Now, did any of you want to go to the store, or should I send someone with a list? Your choice."

"Actually," I said, shocking everyone by speaking up. "I need to go. I just found out from Doc that Trixie has no toys. And her only clothes are pretty much hand-me-downs from her old den. I want to go get her some things of her own."

Owen nodded, leaning down to kiss that soft, little cheek again. "Then yeah, we definitely need to go shopping. Should we take Trixie, let her pick stuff out for her new room? Maybe model some pretty dresses for us?"

I looked him like he'd grown a second head, then turned to Karl for help. Karl was laughing, and shaking his head. Doc rescued us, by speaking up.

"Perhaps it would be best if Miss Trixie finished her nap in the bed that I've been having her use in my quarters upstairs? I believe that your mates are amused by the idea of taking a cub to a store when toys are involved, yes?"

Owen rolled his eyes again. "Seriously? That's your problem? I can handle a cub in a store, how much trouble could that possibly be? She's young."

I snorted, and allowed Karl to field that one. "We shall try that another day, my love. Today, we have no safety seat for the cub. It will be faster, Owen. I do promise that we will make certain to give you the opportunity to take the cub shopping one day soon, yes?"

Jake and I exchanged an amused glance, fully knowing what kind of hell that Owen was setting himself up for if he took the cub shopping.

Unable to resist, I said to Karl, "You know what? We'll get

that car seat installed, and take her to the mall. We can leave her and Owen in the toy store, while you and I stroll around and look at baby stuff."

Karl's eyes twinkled, knowing full well what I was suggesting. Owen, still determined that he could handle a cub in a toy store, nodded emphatically. "Now that sounds like a solid plan! I'll be looking forward to it. But don't be jealous later when I'm her favorite dad after we go."

Doc reached out to take Trixie from Owen, obviously fighting a smile of his own, but wisely staying out of it. Daniel and Jake helped Karl unload the SUV. After it was empty, Karl tossed Owen the keys, and went off with the Alpha to get the key to our new cabin. It was decided that Owen and I would handle the shopping trip.

We were back a few hours later with a newly installed safety seat, and everything we needed for her room. She also had new clothes, books, and toys, even a dolly and an adorable teddy bear. After shopping with Owen, I was worried about letting him shop alone with Trixie. That could actually be a very bad idea. I'd realized this after watching Owen go nuts in the toy section.

CHAPTER 9

T he look on Trixie's face when we introduced her to her new room was priceless. Luckily, I was the kind of dad that already had my phone out recording it. I had fallen instantly in love with this little cub, and I loved watching her react to her new digs.

I knew from my own experience that it would take her a while to settle in and accept that we weren't going anywhere. The poor cub had experienced too much loss already in her life.

Maybe I reacted so strongly to her because I empathized with her situation. It could also be because she looked and smelled just like my alpha mate. Even down to that adorable fucking dimple and those cool copper lines highlighting their gray-green eyes.

It didn't matter why, I just knew that she would never have to doubt that we loved her. She went over and sat down at the cute little white table that I'd found for her. Perched on the tiny ladder-back chair, she looked like a little ray of sunshine. My little sunshine.

I walked over and sat down on the floor beside her, reaching behind her for the tea set that Zane had insisted she needed. Yeah, he could give me the side-eye all he wanted when I talked about spoiling her, but that little shit was right there with me.

I grinned as Gingersnap walked over and sat down across from me, reaching out to distribute little pink teacups to each of us. Karl's rumbling laugh filled the room.

"Uncle Karl, you will also join us for our tea party, yes?"

My big teddy bear was no match for that. He ended up right down there on the floor with us, drinking imaginary tea like a bunch of bosses. After a while, Zane and Karl left us to go do dumb grown-up stuff like fixing our family dinner.

I sat there and played with my sunshine until Karl called us to the table. We had put puzzles together, played with her new dollhouse, and changed the clothes on her new dolly. I didn't give two fucks what we did, I just loved being with my little sunshine.

"Uncle Karl? May I ask a question?"

"Of course, Trixie-bell. You can ask me anything."

"Am I really going to live here forever? Are you guys gonna die?"

Zane's eyes filled, and I reached over to grip his hand in mine while Karl calmed himself to answer.

"Trixie, we do not know how long a person will live, or when they will die. All I can promise is that we are together, and that we will be a family from now on. You do not need to worry about one of us dying. All you need to worry about is being a good cub, eating your vegetables, and picking up your toys, yes?"

Trixie nodded solemnly. "I will be a good cub, Uncle Karl. I promise."

Fuck me. This cub was killing me. I reached over and ruffled her curls. I knew from personal experience what the cub was really asking, but didn't know how to say.

"Trixie, it doesn't matter if you're good or not, we will always love you no matter what. You should be a good girl, because you want to obey us. But not because you think that we will leave you, okay? Cuz trust me, sunshine, that won't ever happen. This is your family now. I promise."

Trixie looked over at Zane for confirmation. He got out of his chair and went over to her. He squatted down at her level, looked her in the eyes, and said, "We promise, Trixie. We are your forever family. And you can't do anything about it, so don't even try!" With that, he tickled her tummy, making her giggle.

Karl and I exchanged a look, both of us loving to see how good Zane was with her. Earlier when Karl had needed one of us, Zane had not hesitated to turn him over to me, while he saw to the cub. I knew that nurturing and compassion were considered to be omega traits, but I think it had more to do with the fact that Zane knew what loss felt like.

* * *

The next month flew by, and Trixie was comfortably settled in with us now. She had nightmares here and there, but one of us was always there to soothe her through it. I hadn't understood why fate had put me together with another alpha. Then an omega had fallen into my lap that I hadn't even wanted, but now here we were, totally perfect together.

We each filled a different role that the others needed, and combined, we were just what Trixie needed. Karl was the one who loved to cook for us, and make sure that we all had everything we needed. He was supportive, patient, and always seemed to know what one of us needed before we knew it ourselves.

My snarky little Gingersnap was the nurturer. He cared for Trixie like she was his own cub. He was right there when one of us needed a hug, and brought balance between me and Karl.

Our sex life had been rough and even slightly competitive before Zane. Having an omega softened us both, and now sex was more and more about connecting than just getting off. I mean, we still had crazy fun in the bedroom, but it was never about who the bigger alpha was anymore.

Zane and I both gave Karl the family he craved, with Trixie as the icing on the cake. I was excited for our new baby. Today we were having an ultrasound, and would find out what we are having. Zane said that we could be surprised by whether we got a cub or a pup, but he needed to know if we needed pink or blue onesies.

None of us gave a shit who the sire was; either way, the baby would belong to all of us. We were building a family, and this time, nothing would take it away from any of us.

"Uncle Owen?"

I turned and picked up my little ray of sunshine, spinning her around in a circle over my head. Lowering her, I adjusted the fluffy skirt of her little pink dress, before planting a loud kiss on her cheek.

"Yes, Miss Trixie?"

"You are silly. I was going to ask if I can play with the pups at the lodge today, while Uncle Zane sees about the baby."

Surprised, I asked her, "How do you know about the baby? We haven't told anyone yet."

She shrugged innocently. "Because, silly. I can smell the

pup. She is a girl like me. Is she going to be my sister? Even if she is a wolf, she can still be my sister, right?"

I heard a gasp behind me, and turned to see a pale Karl and an equally shocked Zane.

"Trixie-bell," Karl said calmly, although I could feel his excitement through our bond. "Can you really smell the baby already? At your age? That's amazing, cub! And you can even smell the fact that it is a wolf pup?"

Trixie gave her uncle a long-suffering smile. "Do not be silly, Uncle Karl. You know that we bears can smell these things. And you really shouldn't call my sister an it. That might hurt her feelings if she finds out later that you called her that, yes?"

I chuckled at her reasonable speech. Zane twirled to glare at Karl, his hands automatically going to his hips. "Do you mean to tell me that you've known all this time what kind of baby we were having? Seriously? You bears and your freaky sense of smell! And you kept this from us?"

Karl smiled gently, and reminded Zane that he had wanted to be surprised.

"Yeah, but it's not a surprise when one of us knows."

"True," I said, "but it's still cool to know. Maybe we should skip the doc and hit the mall instead?"

"NO," my mates both said in stereo.

"Do you hear that, Trixie? They won't let us go to the mall."

Trixie shrugged. "That is okay, Uncle Owen. We will just go by ourselves when they are busy one day, yes?"

I grinned and smacked another kiss on her cheek. "That's a great idea, sunshine. Don't let me forget, okay?"

"Do not worry, Uncle Owen. I will not forget."

Zane snorted, and Karl chuckled, shaking his head at me. Karl never teased me about my devotion to our cub. He only commented once that he had always known that I would be like this if I were ever a dad. It had startled me that he'd ever thought about me in those terms before Zane, but I loved that he saw me in such a positive light.

"Uncle Owen? When the baby comes, if she is my sister, does that mean that you guys will be my daddies then?"

I looked at Karl, who nodded encouragement.

"Trixie. We are your uncles, but we love you like daddies. If you want to call us your daddies, you don't have to wait for the baby to be here, sunshine. It's up to you, but you can call us Daddy whenever you want."

"Alright. Well, I have given it some thought. My friends all have two dads. I can have three. That is okay, because I like all of you. The only problem is that I cannot call all of you the same thing, or you will all answer, yes?"

I chuckled, loving her thought processes. I was

pretty sure that our cub was a genius, but Micah always told me I was prejudiced because his pups were the genius ones. He was wrong though. Miss Sunshine was the smartest little shit that I'd ever met.

"Well," Zane said thoughtfully. "You could call us different names? Like Dad, Daddy, or Papa?"

"What will my sister call you?"

"Whatever you do, sunshine. You get to decide the names, because you got here first."

Liking my answer, Trixie smiled at me. Then she said, "Okay. I know. You and Uncle Zane can be Daddy Owen and Daddy Zane. But I think Uncle Karl should be Papa Karl."

"Why does he get a special name? Do you like him better than me?" I said with a pretend pout.

"Of course not, silly! But Papa Karl is a bear, and we need to remember that, yes?"

"Why, baby?" Zane asked curiously, coming over to tickle her belly.

"Because there are not many bears here, but a lot of wolves. We need to let my sister know that bears are special too."

"Can't argue with that logic," I said. I was relieved that she was honoring her bear heritage, rather than singling it out. I don't know why I worried, she was a smart cub. A little genius.

Zane took off suddenly, rushing for the bathroom.

"Uh-oh. My sister is making Daddy Zane throw up again."

"Yep, she sure is, isn't she?"

* * *

That night, we were cuddling in bed after Trixie was sound asleep. Zane was gushing about his doctor visit, and about how Doc had confirmed what Trixie had told us.

Karl was in the middle, with Zane and I curled up on either side of him. I lifted up and kissed Karl lightly on the lips, leaning over him with my weight on my elbow.

"Does it bother you, babe? That the pup is mine?"

Karl looked at me with surprise. "Why would it? Would it bother you if she were my cub?

"Fuck no. I love you, you're my mate. Any cub of yours would be a cub of mine, right?"

"Ah, so you have answered your own question, yes?"

I grinned, more than a little embarrassed when he put it that way. Zane sat up and crawled up on top of Karl, pushing his leg in carefully between where my body was pressed against Karl's.

"What are you doing, sweetness?" Karl asked, when Zane scraped his teeth along Karl's alpha gland.

"I'm ending this conversation. This is our only grown-up time. I have two alphas, yet the only time I got off this week was from my own hand."

Karl grinned up at Zane, who was leaning over him and planting kisses all over his face.

"Hey, Owen?" Karl asked, as he cupped Zane's little bare ass.

"Yeah, babe?"

"Do you recall giving our omega permission to get off without one of us there to enjoy it?"

"Fuck no. You know what, Gingersnap? I'm a little pissed, now that I think of it. You denied one of us the pleasure of at least watching you work your dick, and maybe even tasting a little of your sweet juices."

Zane giggled, sitting up to jerk his meat. Karl's huge hard-on showed that he was enjoying the show as much as I was. Zane slowly pulled on his cock, while reaching up with his other hand to pinch his nipple. Smelling his slick, I sat up to see the tell-tale glaze coating Karl's abdomen under Zane's ass.

"Hey, Karl. I have a question for you, babe."

"Yes, my love?"

"Your knot or mine?"

"Ooh, tempting. Hmm. Why don't you take him tonight, and let me watch?"

"Do I get a say in this? Maybe I want to choose which knot I ride."

"Hush, Gingersnap. You lost the right to pick when you jerked off without letting us watch."

"Dude. Did you ever hear of consent?"

"Hey, Gingersnap?"

"Yeah, babe?"

"May I please shove my hard cock into your hot ass?"

"Why yes, babe. That sounds like fun. Thank you for asking."

Karl shook his head at us, his big hands stroking Zane's taut cheeks. I moved around, and sat between Karl's legs. He pulled up his knees, spreading them to give me room to join them.

"Ready, my love?"

"Oh, yeah."

Stroking my man-meat, I watched as Karl used his big hands to pull Zane's cheeks open. I watched as he shoved both thumbs inside that hole. I bit down on my lip, loving the view. Karl's big thumbs working Zane's hole was hot as fuck.

"He's all yours, Owen."

I got up on my knees. Karl pulled his hands away as I gripped Zane by the hips. Lining myself up with his hole, I slipped right in when he pushed back against me. I slid my right hand under his chest and pulled him upright with his back to my chest.

Karl sat up to watch. He helpfully guided Zane's legs to straddle the outsides of mine. Kneeling like that, we began to move.

I kept my hand in place, holding him firmly against me as I rocked in and out of his slick channel. He moaned loudly when the fat mushroom head of my cock rubbed against his magic spot. We slowly rocked against each other, enjoying the connection.

Karl got up on his knees, facing us. Leaning across Zane, he kissed me. I nipped at his lip, then sucked his tongue into my mouth. Our tongues danced together, while my hips kept a steady rhythm.

Pulling away, Karl kissed Zane next. I watched them kiss, and began to fuck Zane harder. I held him in place with a firm grip of his hips. I thrust faster now, rocking back slowly then slamming back in.

My knot began to expand at the root of my cock. Working in and out of him, my knot grew fatter. I finally slowed to shallow thrusts when my knot swelled too big to pull out. The pressure of my knot against his magic spot had Zane ready to explode.

"Wait, sweetness. I have an idea that I think you may enjoy, yes?"

"Yes, anything. Just make me come, alpha."

Karl pulled his foreskin out. It was roomy and meaty enough to make a comfortable cradle for Zane's dick. Karl stretched it out with his fingers while Zane moved his dickhead inside the dock. Their dickheads touched. It was raw sex times two, and the dickheads spread slippery pre-cum as Karl frantically rubbed them against each other.

Watching this over Zane's shoulder made me come. I shot spurts of hot cum up inside of his body. My knot engorged fully then. The pressure of the hot walls pressing around my knot made me see stars. I panted for breath, my legs shaking as I tried to keep the two of us upright.

Seconds later, Zane came, biting his fist to muffle his shouts. Karl kept rubbing their dickheads together, even as Zane's cream seeped out of his foreskin, coating his hand.

Karl's head rolled back, his eyes closed in ecstasy. A long groan came from his open mouth as he pulled his dick free of the docking. Holding his huge cock with both hands, Karl opened his eyes and sprayed thick ropes of cum across Zane's chest.

One huge splat shot up and landed on his shoulder. I tipped my face down, looking up at Karl from under my lashes. While he watched, I flicked out my tongue, lapping up his cream.

Reaching out, Karl ran a finger through the pearly honey on Zane's chest

"Open up, sweetness."

Karl fed his cream into Zane's mouth. So fucking hot. I put my hand on Zane's chin, turning his face to mine. Leaning in for a kiss, I savored the flavor of Karl's juices on his tongue.

My legs were cramping now, and I needed to lie down. Wrapping my arms firmly around Zane, I leaned sideways and lowered us to the bed. Finally being able to stretch my legs was heaven after that workout. Zane wriggled on my knot, tugging it slightly as he got comfortable.

We all knew it would take a while for my knot to subside, so we settled in for the night. I knew from experience now that I would eventually slip out of him in our sleep. Until then, we were locked together. I closed my eyes as Karl got up and left the room.

I was dozing lightly, when I felt the bed move. Blinking, I watched as Karl wiped Zane clean with a damp towel, while he snored lightly against my chest. Karl tossed the towel into our hamper, and turned off our bedroom light. The bed dipped when he laid down behind me.

Karl pulled the blanket up over the three of us. His arm came across my waist, his hand resting on Zane's tiny baby bump. I drifted off to sleep thinking how lucky I was to have my mates.

The first two and a half months of Zane's pregnancy had flown by, and aside from swollen ankles, it was surprisingly problem free. The past three weeks though? These had been hell for all of us. Even poor little Trixie looked like she needed a vacation from her grumpy omega daddy.

In his defense, Zane was a week overdue now. Our stubborn pup seemed to be in no hurry to make her appearance. With every passing day, his belly grew larger and his mood got darker. At this point, Owen liked to joke that his belly looked like he had a beach ball shoved under his shirt. Zane wasn't amused. Nothing amused him anymore.

He was stuck in bed, and bored. That was his problem. Every afternoon, Trixie would sit on our bed with him and visit after her nap until dinner. They worked on puzzles, colored with crayons, read stories, and did any other number of quiet activities.

Owen did his patrols during the afternoons, while I ran the woods in the early mornings. Daniel had wanted to give us these last weeks off altogether, but we needed the release that we got from the exercise.

I was just putting dinner on the table, and setting a plate aside for Zane, when Trixie came running into the kitchen.

"Papa! Daddy Zane says that you must fetch Doctor Ollie now. It is time to meet my sister, yes?"

Thankfully, Owen came walking in right then. He took one look at me, and took over. One thing about my alpha mate, he was much better in an emergency than I was. I may have been larger, but he thought faster on his feet. When it came to our family, I tended to freeze under fire.

"Karl, you and Trixie go get Doc. I'll wait here until he arrives, then meet you at the lodge."

"The lodge?" I asked, lost for a moment.

"Yeah, babe. Remember? We can't be here during delivery, that's Doc's rule. We agreed to it, babe. Get a hold of yourself, and stay with me here. No zoning out right now."

Shaking my head, I tried to get with it. "Yes, my love. You are right. I do not wish to wait at the lodge though. It is too far."

"I know, babe. But we still need to get Trixie up to the lodge, she will have a sleepover with the pups up there while we wait."

Zane shouted at us from the bedroom. "Can you figure your shit out *after* you get Doc for me? I'm about to have a tiny human come out of my fucking body and you two ladies are gossiping and planning your evening? Seriously? Are you completely shitting me right now?"

Owen grinned, and took Trixie's hand. "Come on, cub. Let's go play with your friends and find Doc for Daddy Zane. What do you say?"

"Daddy Zane said a bad word."

"Yep, he sure did. Daddy Zane doesn't feel good right now. He'll be better tomorrow, you'll see."

"When my sister is here?"

"Exactly, sunshine. Now let's get going before we get in trouble again. Karl, you wait here," Owen said.

CHAPTER 11

OWEN

I put Trixie on my shoulders so that I could move faster. Once I saw that Doc's lights were off, I made a beeline for the lodge. Doc grabbed his bag when he saw us, and headed straight for our cabin, with Luke and Kai along to assist.

Aries greeted me with a hug, then took Trixie upstairs to play with the pups. I looked around, and saw Daniel sitting over by the big fireplace. I went over and sat down on the couch across from him.

"So, it's finally time, huh?"

"Yeah, can you believe I'm actually going to be a father? I mean, I already am to Trixie, but this time it will be with a brand-new pup. How the fuck am I going to learn to change diapers?"

"Very carefully, especially if they stink," Micah said, as he plopped down next to me. "Congratulations, by the way. I can't believe you knocked up Zany. That's still crazy to me."

I looked at him with a raised brow. "Seriously? Tommy's little brother settles down with two mates, and your only comment is that he got pregnant?"

Micah grinned. "Yeah, I keep myself entertained by imagining Tommy's face if he knew that you and Zany were fated-mates, with another dude along for the ride."

I smacked him in the back of the head, while Daniel watched with a grin. "Shut up, Micah. I know that you knew him as a kid, but he's my mate and so is Karl. My wolf gets pissed when you joke like that."

"Your wolf can suck my fat titty. You know I'm only fucking with you." He looked at me seriously for a second. "You do know that, right? We all like Karl, and we really like the way that you are now that you are with both of them."

I nodded. "I know, I know. You guys wouldn't fuck with my head, you'd say it to my face if you had a problem. Thank you, by the way, for saying that. I like who I am with my mates too."

Daniel smiled wistfully. "I've heard that mates have a way of affecting people like that."

I winced with understanding. "Don't worry, Daniel. When you least expect it, your mate will appear. That's how I met both of mine. I was minding my own business, and fate dropped them in my lap."

Micah elbowed me, "I still can't believe you kept your thing with Karl a secret for over two years. Seriously? Did you really not trust us?"

I shrugged. "I'd never heard of two alphas mating before, I figured maybe there was something wrong with me. It wasn't until Zane entered the picture that the pattern made sense."

Daniel sighed. "Well, I hope that if I have a mate, I can meet him or her soon. I don't mind as a rule, but times like this? It reminds me of what I'm missing in my own life."

I nodded, then sat up as it dawned on me that Karl wasn't here. Shaking my head, I said: "Sorry, guys. We either have to take this conversation outside, or I have to run."

"Why?" Micah asked curiously. "Don't you know Doc's rule?"

"Yeah, I know. But I think that my alpha-mate is choosing to ignore it. Or standing guard at the door. His ass should have been here a long time ago."

My buddies laughed as we all got up to go find my missing mate. It didn't take long. As I'd suspected, there was a very large bear lying in front of our front door. I took one look at him and turned to my friends.

"Sorry guys. There's no way that he's moving. He's settled in for the duration, I know that look in his eyes."

Micah said: "You sure? We could go for a run?"

I thought for a moment, then shook my head. "I'd better not. I should keep Karl company and out of trouble."

They both grinned and congratulated me again before heading back in the direction of the lodge. With a light sigh, I went over to join my mate. It was going to be a long night.

Stripping down, I set my clothes to the side and shifted to my wolf form. I padded across the porch and dropped down gracefully beside Karl's big bear. I snuggled up against his larger form, tucking my head beneath his chin. It would be a long night, but at least in this form, we wouldn't be cold.

CHAPTER 12

KARL

The door opened a little after sunrise. By that time, we had both shifted back and had just gotten dressed again.

Kai put a hand on his hip and smirked up at both of us. "Don't think that I didn't smell your mangy asses out here all night, Owen."

Owen grinned down at him, "Sorry, dude. I couldn't get the big guy here to leave, and I figured it was safer if I stayed to guard him."

Kai shook his head, then stepped forward to give him a hug. "Congrats, Owen. I'm so glad to see you happy now. This has been a long time coming for you, and I am just totally thrilled to see it. Now, get in there and go meet your daughter."

Stepping around him, Kai gave me a big hug too. He said:

"Karl, I'm so glad that you're part of our pack now to stay. Your little Trixie is an amazing cub! Is it rude if I ask her designation?"

I smiled proudly, always ready to brag about Trixie. Owen smiled right along with me, equally proud of our cub. "Actually, this may surprise you. Trixie is an omega."

"Seriously? I totally had her pegged as alpha! She's just so logical and decisive, you know?" Kai rambled, but I could tell that he had honestly been thinking about it.

"Ah. Well, bear omegas are slightly different in their natures. It may shock you, but they are usually the bossy ones in our dens."

Kai grinned. "That doesn't shock me a bit! Most alphas just don't like to admit who really run things, right?"

I smiled back at him, but then I remembered. Our omega and pup were waiting inside! I pulled Owen's hand and tugged him into our cabin with me. I said over my shoulder to Kai: "Please forgive my rudeness, Kai. I just remembered that our mate and pup are still waiting in there to meet us, yes?"

Kai nodded with a knowing smile. "No worries, get in there."

We went.

When I walked into the room, the first thing that I noticed was Zane's glowing face. Always beautiful, his porcelain skin looked dew-kissed, after his night of exertion.

Owen released my hand and went over to the bed. He sat down next to Zane. After kissing his freckled cheek, Owen bent over to look at the bundle in our mate's arms.

Spurred into movement, I went over and sat at the other side of Zane. I also kissed his cheek first, then gazed down at the bundle. Transfixed, I could not take my eyes away from her.

Owen laughed, looking at me over Zane's head. "Can you believe that our Gingersnap gave us a mini-gingersnap? Figures, right?"

Looking up at us, was a tiny little creature with a shock of orange red hair sticking up in all directions on the top of her head. I bit my lip to hold in my chuckle, but it didn't work.

Owen made the mistake of snorting, and then I lost all control. We sat there, looking at the nearly translucent white skin of the prettiest little baby girl. Her gorgeous green eyes were so dark, they were almost the color of the pines in our forest. But that hair! My goodness, I had never seen such crazy hair on a child before, let alone a newborn babe.

We laughed until we cried, and then Zane's glares made us laugh some more. Once I had calmed down, I leaned over to kiss my mate's cheek again. He jerked away, cuddling the pup close to his chest.

"Seriously? You fuckers just laughed at our new pup, and now you want to kiss me? What the hell, Karl? You're supposed to be the sane one around here!"

"Shit, you should have seen him last night, if you think that. Gingersnap, you would have laughed. He kept freezing up, forgetting what he was doing, like he was in a fugue state or something. Our big bear just doesn't do well in an emergency, I hate to break it to you."

"Excuse me, but I was concerned for our mate. Child-birth is hard work."

"Yep, that's why they call it labor," quipped Zane.

I turned to Zane. "Sweetest, I promise you that I was not laughing at our child. It was just the contrast of her perfect little angel face and delicate skin tone, and then that crazy head of hair sticking out every which way. Also, I did not sleep last night, so I am not quite myself just now. I could not help it, yes?"

Zane looked at me lovingly and leaned over to meet me for a kiss. "I get it. I've been trying to smooth that hair down while I waited for you, but the more I brush it down, the faster it pops up. I just hope it turns to curls as it gets longer. I don't want our little Ava to walk around looking like she stuck a wet finger in an electric socket for her entire life, right?"

I cleared my throat, trying not to laugh at Zane's amusing depiction. "Ava? This is what you wish to name our daughter, yes?"

"Oh, crap! I forgot to tell you guys the name I settled on? I'm such a dick!"

"Naw, but you do have one. A kinda cute one too, if I remember right." Owen said with a wink.

Zane rolled his eyes, but his cheeks blushed, betraying his emotion.

"So, yeah. What do you guys think? Ava?"

"I like it, sweetest. Ava, our angel."

Owen nodded, grinning down at our crazy-haired pup. "Yeah, but I'm totally calling her Carrots, since Ginger-snap is already taken."

Before Zane could get upset again, we heard the front door open. Trixie's chatter could be heard above the adult voice of whoever had escorted her home. Her little face peeked around the edge of the door-frame a few moments later.

"Hello, Trixie-bell. Have you come to meet your sister?"

Trixie nodded shyly. "I would like to meet her, yes?"

"Yes," Zane said, shifting the pup into Owen's arms and reaching out for Trixie to come to him. "Get over here and give me a hug first, and quit being such a silly little weirdo."

Trixie relaxed her stiff posture and climbed up to give her daddy a hug. "I am happy that my sister is here, Daddy Zane. I am still to be her sister, yes?"

Zane leaned back, and looked her in the eyes, holding her little hands in his own. "Trixie, girl. Remember what we told you when you came to live with us? That we are your forever family?"

Trixie nodded, her green eyes huge in her tiny face.

"Well, pretty girl, forever means that it never ends. This will always be your home, and you will always be our daughter. No matter how many pups or cubs we have in the future, you will always be our oldest daughter. Now, tell me. How will your little sister learn to be a smart cookie if she doesn't have a big sister to teach her?"

Trixie's face lit up. "Well, I did not have a big sister to show me. I had to learn it for myself. But, then. I am a bear. We are stronger, yes? I will teach my sister to be strong like a bear."

I leaned over and kissed her chubby little cheek. I could not believe that I had been blessed with two wonderful mates, and now, two beautiful daughters. We had all come from different places and backgrounds, but we had all been lonely, even in a crowd. Together now, we would never be lonely again, and neither would our daughters.

Owen brought the baby close for Trixie to admire. "Hey, sunshine. Meet your sister, Ava. Or as I like to call her, Carrots."

Trixie giggled when she saw Ava's hair. She looked up at my alpha-mate and said: "I agree, Daddy Owen. Her name has to be Carrots, yes?"

"Yes," Owen and I said together, while Zane rolled his eyes and grinned.

Fin

What happens when your fated mate is also your natural predator?

Join my mailing list and get your FREE copy of The Rabbit Chase

https://dl.bookfunnel.com/vfk1sa9pu3

Twitter:
https://twitter.com/SusiHawkeAuthor

Facebook:
https://www.facebook.com/SusiHawkeAuthor

ALSO BY SUSI HAWKE

Northern Lodge Pack Series

Omega Stolen: Book 1

Omega Remembered: Book 2

Omega Healed: Book 3

Omega Shared: Book 4

Omega Matured: Book 5

Omega Accepted: Book 6

Omega Grown: Book 7

Northern Pines Den Series

Alpha's Heart: Book 1

Alpha's Mates: Book 2

Alpha's Strength: Book 3

Alpha's Wolf: Book 4

Alpha's Redemption: Book 5

Alpha's Solstice: Book 6

Blood Legacy Chronicles

Alpha's Dream: Book 1

Non-Shifter Contemporary Mpreg

Pumpkin Spiced Omega: The Hollydale Omegas - Book 1

Cinnamon Spiced Omega: The Hollydale Omegas - Book 2

Peppermint Spiced Omega: The Hollydale Omegas - Book 3

Made in the USA
Coppell, TX
13 March 2022

74897520R00090